Key

Perhaps buried in the castle too

A sharp key, maybe too sharp or alternatively it may be flat

For a wild test eat thirty

Part of the last will. I am sure that you will find what you're looking for if you ask politely

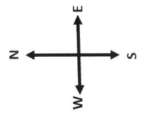

Chapter 1 Parliament Street

Some people can't see what's happening around them. Or maybe they just don't look.

*

Claudia Ding stepped off the 415 bus and scanned the area around her. Everywhere she looked people were rushing through life, completely lost in their own world. A tall man with blonde hair and a thick beard hurried by her looking firmly towards the ground. Two young women walked down the street towards her, hand in hand and unable to keep their eyes off each other. A family on the other side of the street were taking their puppy for a walk, cooing and giggling every time he did something adorable.

"Mum"

"Hmmmmmm"

"Can we go to a café for lunch?"

"What's that honey?"

"Can we go to a café for lunch?"

"Hang on Claudia, I've just got to reply to this text….OK, now what were you saying?"

"Can we get lunch in a café today? It would be nice to have proper tea and cakes whilst we're in town."

"Maybe honey, if we've got time."

That meant no.

"But we've got a lot to do today." Her Mother continued. "We'll have fun though won't we?"

"Yeah of course."

Even at her tender young age, Claudia knew when it was better to tell white lies rather than crush someone with the truth. Was it really fun anymore? Tramping around the city centre of York every Saturday was not exactly her idea of fun. Claudia's Mother reached out to try and hold hands with Claudia but found her daughter pulling her own hand away in rejection.

First task was (as ever) to hike up Parliament Street to make their weekly deposit to the bank. Parliament Street was one of the main shopping streets in York. Created in the 19th Century by demolishing a load of smaller medieval lanes, the street was unnecessarily wide and lined with large shops and major banks. Despite the street's width it was (as ever) absolutely rammed with bodies. There were hundreds of people going back and forth, bumping into one another and all reluctantly sharing the space with strangers that they were barely willing to acknowledge or even notice.

Claudia noticed though. She noticed all of the shoppers laden with heavy bags as they heaved and puffed their way back to their cars. She noticed all of the teenagers, hanging around and desperately trying to look cool in front of their mates. She noticed the bored family members following their more enthusiastic loved ones around the city. She even noticed the woman with long black hair and a long black coat who appeared to be watching Claudia and her mother as they hurried up the street after having left the bank.

They headed up Parliament Street then Davygate and Blake Street before turning left onto Museum Street and towards their next stop at the library. The trip to the library which was always the best part of Saturday, her mother gave a weekly lecture on local history and whilst that was going on Claudia got to amuse herself among the books and speak to her friend Lucy Cavendish.

Claudia had no idea how old Lucy was, she looked young to Claudia but her mother always said that Lucy had been working at the library for as long as anyone could remember. Either way, she was friendly and interesting and always talked to Claudia when she visited.

"Claudia, how are you this fine Saturday morning" Lucy Cavendish was a bright and cheery as ever.

"Oh fine. Happy to be here." Claudia replied mustering as much enthusiasm as she could manage.

"What's your mum's talk on today?"

"Oh something about some Viking or other who got killed by being thrown in a pit of snakes."

"Well that sounds exciting."

Lucy's enthusiasm was not well received. Claudia looked at Lucy with scorn, raised an eyebrow and sighed

"I take it you won't be sitting in on the talk then" Lucy continued with a smile

"What's the point? It's all boring." Claudia was really nailing the sceptical look.

"You don't think this Viking chap and the pit of snakes sounds exciting?"

Claudia raised her other eyebrow in an attempt to look even more doubtful. She then realised that with both eyebrows raised she no longer looked sceptical, now she just looked surprised. She lowered her brow and sighed.

"There are no pits of snakes in York. There never has been and there never will be." Claudia said.

"Oh well, lots of books in here for you to explore if you want. We'll leave your mother to local history and if you change your mind and decide you want to get interested in it then there are loads of good things to read."

"That's another thing that will never happen, me getting interested in local history."

"But York has got all of these wonderful stories." Lucy tried again hopefully "Roman, Viking, Anglo-Saxon, Norman, and Medieval." Lucy could tell that she was losing this battle.

"Yes I know, Mum keeps banging on about it. Capital of the North and all that. The only interesting thing she's ever told me is that there was a Legion of 5,000 Roman soldiers that lived here and they were the men who built Hadrian's Wall. And now I say that out loud even that doesn't sound very interesting."

"Ok Claudia, well you find yourself a nice book to read and leave all the boring history stuff to your mum."

It was a pity that Claudia had no interest in learning about the history of York because it really was a belter of a place. A bustling, modern, exciting city still surrounded by the high, thick stone city walls built 800 years earlier. The centre of the city was a mixture of small, narrow, ancient streets and large, impressive buildings.

The most impressive of all was York Minster, a giant medieval cathedral that still dominated the city skyline. Rising above the surrounding buildings like a stately ship soaring above the waves in the ocean. The Minster was built in the shape of a cross measuring 160 metres long and 70 metres across, each arm of the cross was an impressive 30 metres wide and 30 metres high with 3 towers raising above the building reaching up to a height of 70 metres. In total it took over 250 years to build this massive undertaking with the intricately cut stonework and painstakingly worked stained glass all manufactured and installed by hand.

Every time Claudia walked past The Minster she was amazed by all the people who had travelled miles and miles to come and gawp at it. She heard accents from all over England, Scotland, Wales and Ireland as well as Canadian, New Zealand, American and Australian voices. She heard people speaking French, Spanish, German and Italian and was fascinated by the groups of people listening to tour guides speaking Russian, Mandarin and Japanese. And always, always, there were groups of young people trying desperately to take photos of themselves with as much of The Minster as they could fit in the background. Even now towards the end of the summer tourism season there were still hordes of visitors all clustering around the place. It was like all of the world had descended on a small part of Northern England, and Claudia loved it.

But Claudia and her Mother weren't stopping at The Minster. The two of them hurried down the street called Low Petergate into Kings Square, tantalisingly within distance of many wonderful looking cafes, before turning left onto St. Andrewgate. Due to a historical quirk, several street names in York had the word gate in them, Claudia's mother said it was something to do with the Vikings but Claudia never really understood why.

They rang the doorbell of Mr Barry's house and hoped that the previous lesson wasn't overrunning. Claudia's piano teacher had a lot of qualities but punctuality was not one of them, an irony that was not lost on Claudia every time she was told off for not keeping to time. Claudia looked around and scanned the street once more looking for anything interesting to occupy her. As she turned around something caught her attention on the balcony of an opposite building. Something was moving, something small and dark creeping carefully along the railings of the balcony. Claudia took a closer look and realised it was a black cat, keeping it's shoulders low to avoid detection and slowly putting one paw in front of the other as if it was stalking something. Claudia followed the cat's gaze and saw a second, smaller black cat on the roof of the next door building. Was this an invader that the stalking cat was looking to see off? Maybe they were just siblings playing a game. Either way, something exciting was going to happen.

"Mum, have a look at those cats on the balconies, I think there is going to be a fight." Claudia said excitedly

"What cats?" her mother replied. "Oh those are just statues honey. Don't you remember when we went around York and found all the cat statutes on the buildings? Didn't we decide there was about 30 of them in total? There are a couple of them in Kings Square as well."

What was she talking about? These weren't statues, they were moving and stalking and....oh no as Claudia looked again they weren't moving at all. They were statues and they were stood motionless on the building. Why did she think that they had been moving? It was very odd.

The door opened and Mr Barry's cheery face greeted them

"Ah Claudia, good to see you." He said with a smile "Right, let's learn some piano."

Chapter 2 Kings Square

"Have you found them?"

"Not yet My Lady but I will."

"Find them NOW. No more excuses."

*

Claudia and her mother left Mr Barry's house and made their way back towards Kings Square. Despite the name, Kings Square wasn't really a square. It was more of a triangle but it did act as a nice open space for tourists to gather and street performers to try and drum up some cash. On this day there was an escapologist performing on the raised area at the wide end of the triangle. Claudia had seen him there before, in fact although she had never stopped to watch his act, she had seen so much of it a bit at a time that she reckoned that she knew it word for word.

She looked around for anything else that she might find interesting. Sure enough, on the roof of the pub behind the escapologist she could see another statue of a cat. This one was designed to look like it was stalking a small bird on the roof, which was of course also a statue. Elsewhere there were people buying ice cream from a tall and thin young man in an ice-cream cart and also....there she was again, the woman in the long black coat looking towards Claudia and her mother. Was this the same woman as before? She certainly looked like it. And whoever she was she was definitely watching Claudia and her mother, following what they were doing. Claudia looked up at her mother but saw that she was lost in her own thoughts and clearly hadn't seen the woman. Claudia looked back across the square and found herself making eye contact with the woman. A small smile appeared on the Woman in Black's lips.

"Hello...it's OK. Come closer."

The woman was not shouting, she was speaking softly but clearly. Claudia realised she could only hear this one clear voice despite all of the other people in the square. She could hear no tourists, no shoppers and no street performers repeating their long worn out jokes. She could only hear that one woman in the long black coat.

"It's OK. Come closer." The woman repeated.

Claudia looked back up to see her mother's reaction. Her mother didn't look surprised or annoyed she just looked...blank. Completely unaware of anything that was going on. In fact she wasn't moving at all, she was entirely rigid, frozen completely motionless. Slowly Claudia looked around the square and sure enough everyone in there was entirely frozen in time.

"It's OK. Come closer." The lady in the long black coat said for third time.

Claudia felt that she had no choice. She left her mother's side and walked over to the other side of the square. She couldn't help but shoot a look back towards her mother.

"It's OK, she's fine. Everyone here is totally fine." The woman was smiling. She seemed reassuring, friendly. Nice even.

"Why aren't they moving?" Claudia asked

"Oh there is nothing wrong with them. They just can't see us."

"How can I see you then?"

"Some people can't see what's happening around them. Or maybe they just don't look. But I knew you were observant from the moment I first glimpsed you. I knew I'd be able to talk to you."

Claudia looked back at her mother again. Her mother was always rushing around, she always had so much to do and was always being distracted by her phone. Maybe she just wasn't looking at the world as closely as Claudia was and that's why she couldn't see this woman. Then as Claudia looked, her mother started to fade from view. In a real panic she looked around the square and saw all of the bodies fading from view.

"It's OK" said the woman warmly "They are absolutely fine. It's just that, well if they can't see us then there is no point in us seeing them. But they aren't going anywhere. Who was that you were stood with?"
"It was my mother."

"All you need to do is come back here and look for your mother and you'll find her easily enough. You're good at looking for things aren't you."
"I don't know."

"Well do you see things that other people can't?"

"I guess so yes." Claudia thought for a second then turned back to look towards St Andrewgate. "Actually I've just seen two cats stalking each other along the balconies back there but my Mum was sure they were just statues."

"Oh those two black cats. They're always at it. But they love each other really. They're brother and sister and are just playing games."

Claudia smiled. She was starting to feel more relaxed. By now all of the people who had been in the square with her had entirely disappeared but she was no longer worried. She felt that she liked the woman in the long black coat.

"My name is Mathilda." Said the woman "What's your name?"

"Claudia Ding."

"What a lovely name. Well Claudia Ding, it is a pleasure to meet you."

"So what is this place then?" Claudia asked. "Where am I?"

"Well you're still in York." Mathilda replied "Just a different version of York. This city has been here for about 2,000 years now and it's seen so many significant and interesting things in that time. All those events, all those buildings, all those people who have been here have left a trace behind, an echo if you like. The trouble is, most people are not able to see those echoes. Only really observant people like you can see them. Do you understand?"

"Yes." Claudia replied confidently.

"Really?" Mathilda probed

"No."

"Don't worry. You'll get used to things soon enough. The main thing is, there is this Echo World. Some people can only see your world, some people can only see this world and a small number of people like you and I can go between the worlds."

"Right. So how do these echoes show themselves?"

"They come and go. One place may have seen lots of different things over the years so sometimes you'll see one thing there and other times you'll see something else. It usually depends on what you're looking for. For example, if you looked over to your right, what would you expect to see?"

"Well, it's the corner or Low Petergate and Goodramgate. There's some shops, a fish and chip restaurant, some cafes."

"Yes. That's one version of what's there. However in this world there are also echoes of things from the past. Have a look, it might look very different to what you'd expect."

Claudia, wasn't convinced. She looked over to her right but was completely expecting to see the shops and restaurants of Low Petergate as usual. But no, sure enough there was no fish and chip restaurant, no cafes, no shops. Instead there was a strong looking stone wall with a tall, powerful looking stone gateway building containing large wooden doors. Along the wall and around the gateway patrolled soldiers wearing shiny metal helmets and armour and carrying large red rectangular shields and fierce looking spears.

"How...when...what..." Claudia was so surprised that she couldn't do anything but ask one word questions.

"It will all seem normal soon enough. Don't worry about it at all." Mathilda was smiling. "They are the Roman soldiers that used to live in York, on this site was one of the gateways into their fortress. Even though the fortress has not been here for 1600 years, for several centuries before that this spot was of huge significance and activity and has left a powerful echo on the city."

"And the echoes are visible in this world?" Claudia asked looking back to Mathilda

"Yes they are. These echoes come and go. What might be there one minute might look very different soon after. Have a look back over there."

Claudia looked back towards the gateway. Sure enough the Roman soldiers had all gone, as had the wall from the fortress. The gateway building was still there though as well as several people walking around. Claudia recognised these people from pictures she has seen in school. The heavy bearskin coats, pointed helmets, circular shields and long swords all pointed to these being Vikings.

"Later on" Mathilda explained "The Viking Kings that ruled York used this Roman gatehouse building as their great hall. And if you look to the left you will see something else."

Claudia looked left and did see something else. At the wide end of Kings Square, on the raised area that she had just seen the escapologist performing, there was now a church. It was a short church only just fitting into the space but unmistakably a church with a familiar tall tower sticking up above the buildings surrounding it.

"That's never been there before." Claudia said in surprise.

"Oh yes it has. Holy Trinity Church stood on that spot from the medieval period until the 1930's."

"And all these things leave echoes in your world?" Claudia was trying to understand everything that was happening. "Why don't we see the echoes in our world?"

"They have left echoes in your world it's just harder for you to see them. You have to be curious and observant to find them. The Roman fortress has long since gone but it still impacts the layout of the streets. People are still walking down the same streets as they were 2000 years ago. They have different names now, the Roman road called Via Principia is now called Petergate and the Via Praetoria is called Stonegate but we but are literally all following in the footsteps of people who came before us. Where we're stood now is called Kings Square, named after the Viking Kings' great hall that was here. The church has long gone but if you look down some of the gravestones have been reused in the pavement. You can still read them as you walk across them."

"And you say that people live in this Echo World?" Claudia asked.

"Yes. Some people can only see this Echo World. I sometimes have trouble making people believe that your own world even exists. But you and I are the special ones. We can see both worlds. It will seem strange at first but before long you'll be able to switch back and forth between worlds in an instant and not think anything of it."

"OK, well that's good. I guess." Claudia said in an unconvincing manner "Will I be able to see your world for the rest of my life?"

"Maybe. Maybe not. It's difficult to tell. Young people are usually the most observant and are best at finding this world. Some of them stop looking for us as they get older but some are able to see properly for the rest of their lives."

"Will my mother miss me while I'm here?"

"She won't even notice you are gone. Time does go by while you're here but not in the same way. You might be with us for an hour or two and your mother might think you've only been gone for a couple of seconds."

Mathilda stopped and looked at Claudia, trying to read her reaction.

"Would you like to go back to your mother now?" Mathilda asked

"Yes please, that would be nice." Claudia replied.

"No problem. When will you next be in the city?"

"We come in every Saturday morning around 10 o'clock on the 415 bus."

"Well I'll look out for you then. Don't forget to look for me."

"Oh I won't."

"Goodbye for now then Claudia Ding. Just go and look for your mother, she'll be there."

"Goodbye Mathilda. I'll see you next week."

Claudia crossed to the other side of the square to the spot she had left her mother. All she had to do was look? It didn't sound likely but she gave a good look and...Oh there her mother was, stood in exactly the same spot as if Claudia had never left her. In fact everyone was exactly the spot they had been before.

"There's no time I'm afraid" Claudia's mother said.

"Sorry?" Claudia's mind was distracted by other things.

"I said there's no time to go to a café for lunch. We'll just have to grab something quick and get on with other things."

"Oh right. Yes that's fine."

The two of them walked off into towards their next task. Shopping. The worst task of all. Soon they would be like all of the other people in York, too busy to notice anything that's going on around them.

"Ladies and gentlemen." The escapologist tried one last time to get people interest in his act "If you just stop and watch for a minute I promise you'll see things that wouldn't believe were possible."

"If only you knew." Thought Claudia. "If only you knew."

Chapter 3 The Shambles

"You will"

"But Your Majesty, I can't'"

"I don't care what you can or can't do Master Mason, you WILL do this."

*

Claudia could barely concentrate all week. She was desperate to get into York again and see Mathilda and the Echo World. The temptation to tell her friends about what had happened was burning but what if they didn't believe her. Even worse, what if she had imagined the whole thing to begin with.

By the time Saturday came again Claudia was beside herself with excitement. She stepped off the 415 bus and looked around triumphantly, fully expecting to see the woman in the long black coat waiting for her. But there was no sign of Mathilda. No sign at all. How disappointing.

"Come on Claudia, we need to get to the bank." Her mother said impatiently
"Hang on a minute. "Claudia replied, still scanning the area in case she had missed her friend.

"What are you waiting for? Come on, we've got a lot of things to do today, no time to stand and stare."
"OK mum, I'm coming."

There was still no sign of Mathilda in Parliament Street, no sign near the library as her mother gave this week's lecture (this week the lecture was on French airman who had apparently saved York during World War 2), no sign of Mathilda near The Minster and no sign of her on their way down to Mr Barry.

By the time she had completed her piano lesson, a very disappointed Claudia Ding had come to the conclusion that she had imagined the whole thing after all. Of course Mathilda didn't exist, of course there wasn't any sort of echo world. Of course it was just the same boring Saturday that she always had. She trudged after her mother, eyes to the ground, not even bothering to look for anything interesting as they reached Kings Square.

"Claudia."

"Yes Mum."

"Claudia."

"What is it?"

She looked up towards her mother with a grumpy sigh, expecting that she would soon have to answer one of those stupid questions that adults like to ask. But it wasn't her mother quizzing her. In fact, her mother was entirely motionless. Frozen to the spot like everyone else around them.

"Claudia, look this way. Over here."

Claudia's head shot around with eyes wide and mouth open. Sure enough, there was the woman with her long black hair and long back coat. Claudia let out an excited gasp.

"Mathilda!" She cried.

"Hi there Claudia. Sorry I missed you earlier but I guessed I could find you here again." Mathilda said with an air of embarrassment.

"No it's fine. I wasn't bothered." Claudia tried desperately to pretend she was laid back and calm. She glanced around her, with as much nonchalance as she could muster. She noticed all of the frozen figures around the square were already beginning to fade from view.

"So do you want me to show you around then?" Mathilda asked awkwardly.

"Yeah. I suppose." Claudia suddenly felt the effort of pretending to be cool was too great to keep up. A large grin broke out across her face. "That would be amazing if you could show me around. Thanks Mathilda. It's good to see you."

With the tension broken, Mathilda led them out of the square with a bounce in their steps and excited smiles.

"Now do you know the name of this street?" Mathilda said as she reached a particularly narrow and picturesque street with old looking buildings overhanging the pavement on either side of the road.

"Yes, it's called The Shambles." Claudia replied "In my world it's always absolutely rammed with tourists."

"Not in this world. It's a working street. So do you know why it's called The Shambles?"

Claudia though back to all of the lectures her mother had given her over the years.

"Butchers" she ventured eventually after a deep think "the butchers lived here. And we use the word shambles to mean a mess because medieval butchers would have been incredibly messy places."

"Excellent knowledge young lady. Somebody has taught you well."

Claudia was losing concentration. She had been down this road many times before but not without hundreds of people down here. She looked up at the buildings either side of the road. They were very old buildings made with timber frames and plaster. Each floor stuck out beyond the floor below so that as the building got higher it just got bigger and bigger. She stood between two buildings and looked up, they seemed to be leaning towards the building on the other side of the road as if leaning into each other with the expectation of a kiss. The buildings were almost touching at the top and even though she was stood in the middle of the road, she could barely see the sky. Claudia felt dizzy looking up at them and turned to face Mathilda again, trying to tune in to what she was talking about.

"...and these shelves outside the butchers are where they place the meat, or flesh as it was also called, so that customers could see what was for sale. An old word for a shelf is a shammel and the shelves outside a butchers used to be called fleshammels and that is where the word shambles comes from.

A man's voice called out to end the impromptu history lesson.

"Is that Mathilda I see standing there? What can I get for you today?"
"Hello there Gus, how's life?" Mathilda replied.

"Oh we keep on keeping on. You know how it is."
"Is your sister around?"

"Meg is around here somewhere but right now she has generously allowed me to do all the work in the shop. And who is this a friend of yours?"

"Of course, how rude of me. This is Claudia Ding. Claudia, this is my friend Gus Montgomery. He's a butcher."

Claudia had already figured out for herself what Gus' job was. The shelf outside the shop, the fleshammel itself, was absolutely heaving with tasty looking meat. There were expertly cut chops, juicy looking steaks and perfectly presented joints of meat on the shelf as well as several bunches of thick, meaty sausages hanging on hooks around the door.

Gus himself looked like a man who enjoyed his food. Certainly he was showing early signs of middle aged spread and his apron, which once may once have fitted perfectly, now hugged his belly very tightly. He had a round, kind looking face that was partly covered by close cropped, dark beard and his hair had distinct patches of grey around the temples.

"Hello there Claudia." Gus said "Can I tempt you with any of our produce here?"

"Well it all looks great..." Claudia shifted awkwardly on the spot "It's just that I'm ... I'm..."

"Vegetarian?" Gus guessed "That is no problem. Step through this doorway and we'll see what we can do for you."

Claudia didn't really see the point of this. She could see inside the butchers shop from where she stood and there certainly wasn't anything inside there for her. But she didn't want to seem impolite and so followed her instructions.

As she stepped through the door she found herself not inside a butchers as she was expecting but inside a café.

"But…what…this isn't a…it's a café. Well that's amazing…where's all the meat gone."

"We're only a butchers if you're looking for a butchers. This building has also been used as a café. If you are looking for a café, then that's what you'll find."

"She's not from this world." Mathilda tried to explain.

"Oh yes, one of Mathilda's friends from the other world. This other world that she assures us we'd be able to see if we just looked carefully. Well you'll find things work differently around here compared to your world."

"But how can all of that meat just disappear?"

"I don't know. It's just the way things work around here."

Claudia still didn't understand what was happening, but then nothing was making a lot of sense right now. Besides, her attention had been taken by something else. A woman had appeared from the back of the shop and was sneaking up behind Gus. She put a finger to her lips as she caught Claudia's eye. Carefully and stealthily she came up and tapped Gus on his right shoulder before immediately ducking around behind him. Gus look to his right with a confused expression only to find no one there. The woman lent into his left ear.

"BOOO" she shouted making Gus nearly jump out of his skin.

"Gah, flipping heck Meg. You'll be the death of me doing that."

Even without introductions Claudia could guess this was Gus' sister. She had the same round, kind face, same reassuring smile and same dark hair as her brother. She didn't seem to have the same appetite however as her apron still fitted perfectly.

"Claudia, this is my sister Meg. Meg, this is Claudia. She is from the other world." Gus eventually said when he'd got his breath back.

"Yes, I heard you speaking when I was in the back. Hello Claudia, welcome to the Echo World. I'm sure you'll have fun here. Now can we get you anything to eat? Free of charge of course."
Claudia chanced her luck. The food looked so nice that it was worth asking for the best.

"Do you have any scones?"

"Do we have any scones she asks? Only the best scones that you'll ever eat. And you'll want a cup of tea to go with that. Well Gus will fix that for you, won't you Gus?" The way Meg spoke, it didn't sound like Gus had much of a choice.

"Of course I will." He replied "It will give me the chance to have sit down get my heartbeat back to normal."

Gus disappeared to the back of the shop and Meg continued the conversation with Claudia.

"So are you new around here?" She asked

"Yes" Claudia replied "This is the first time I've explored this world. It's all very confusing. But exciting as well."

"Well you're always welcome here. Any friend of Mathilda is a friend of ours. We can get pretty busy with the shop but always find time for a friendly face."

Suddenly there was a shriek from outside. Claudia looked out with a start to see a black cat scurrying vertically up the wall opposite them. There was a second sound and she looked up to see another cat, this one fluffy and white and as if made out of wool. The white cat saw the Claudia looking at it and in the panic of the moment collapsed into what appeared to just be a ball of wool left resting on the window ledge. Claudia's eyes bulged as if she was struggling to believe what she had seen.

"Oh they'll be fine, they do it all the time." Meg said reassuringly "Woolcat there will get herself together eventually. You'll get used to all of this sort of thing soon enough."

"Here we go, scone with strawberry jam, clotted cream and a pot of tea." Gus returned from the back of the shop holding what looked to Claudia like a piece of heaven.

She took a bite and it was good. Meg hadn't lied, it really was the best she ever tasted.

"Enjoying it?" Gus asked

"Mmphhhmm" Came the muffled reply through a mouthful of scone.

"Fantastic. Always good to see a satisfied customer."

"So I'm sure Mathilda has told you about the Fleshammels and that's why it is called The Shambles." Meg said to Claudia as she enjoyed her cake "But I can add more to that. Did you know that Kings Square is actually named after Henry VIII's favourite shape."

"Is that true?" Gus asked looking incredulously at Meg "I never knew that."

"Of course that's not true you dullard. You really will believe everything I tell you won't you?"

"Oh. I guess" Gus looked dejected. Claudia couldn't help but laugh.

"And York is actually short for You're Kidding? Which is what the locals always say when they've been told something untrue" Meg looked over at her brother "No? Not going to fall that one? You are getting better at this."

Claudia laughed again. She got the feeling that this was the type of thing that happened frequently with these two. The four of them sat and talked as Claudia finished her scones and tea. Eventually a group of other customers approached the shop.

"Well you're obviously very busy." Mathilda said "We'll leave you to it."

They bid their cheery goodbyes and Claudia and Mathilda headed further down to the end of the street to see what else they could find. They reached the far end of The Shambles and emerged onto the road called. Claudia looked across the street and saw another man standing at the corner of The Stonebow and Fossgate. He seemed to be looking in their direction.

"Is that Mathilda I see?" He spoke in a clear and articulate voice "And who is your young friend?"

"Balthazar. It's been a long time since we last spoke." Mathilda replied as the man crossed the street to speak to them. "This is Claudia Ding, Claudia this man is called Balthazar."

"It's a pleasure to meet you Claudia Ding."

She gave him a good look over. He was tall and slender with a long serious face and the most piercing eyes Claudia had ever seen. He had perfectly white hair like old man but the smooth skin of much younger person. He was wearing long robes and hood of the brilliant white colour that you only usually see on an advert for laundry products. The whole outfit made him look like a wise old monk. She must have been checking him out in a less subtle way than she thought as it was clear that Balthazar had clocked her looking at him.

"I get the impression you enjoy taking close looks at things" He said.

"Oh she is a very observant person." Mathilda replied. "She definitely sees things other people would miss."

"So then, young observant Claudia, what do you see when you look at me?"

Claudia took a good hard look at Balthazar, she wanted to say something intelligent but not insulting. For some reason, she found herself wanting to impress this man.

"You come across as very calm, with an air of authority and wisdom. Someone that people could trust and follow." She was proud of her self so far "However, as I don't know you I have no idea if that is a true impression or not. I also feel that if you wanted to, you could be in a position to exploit this."

For a few seconds Claudia regretted going so far. Her words hung in the air as Balthazar looked at her with his long, impassive face. She wondered if it was possible in this world to grab your words from the air and put them back into your mouth as if you'd never said them. Then, all of a sudden, Balthazar threw back his head and let out a hearty laugh.

"I don't know if people feel that they would follow me." He said through the chuckles. "But I must confess that lots of people see the white hair and long robes and assume that I am much wiser than I actually am. Although, I can assure you young lady that I have never exploited anybody."

Claudia was relieved, she hadn't gone too far after all and Balthazar had taken her observations with good heart.

"It has truly been a pleasure to meet you Claudia." Balthazar said still smiling "Stay observant but maybe do us all a favour and keep your observations to yourself. We don't want you getting yourself into any trouble do we? If you ever want to speak to me then come and look for me around here. I'm sure you'll find me easily enough."

Balthazar nodded a polite goodbye to both Claudia and Mathilda, turned and slowly walked away down Stonebow. As he left, Claudia once again could not help but be reminded of a wise old monk.

"Well it has been fun but have you had enough for today?" Mathilda asked

"Yes I think I have?" Claudia replied, happy but exhausted.

"Time to get back to your mum and your own world?"

"Yes, that would be nice."

The two of them returned to Kings Square. Claudia began walking towards where she had left her mother.

"Goodbye Claudia, remember that I will always be here if you look for me."

"Goodbye Mathilda. Thank you."

Claudia walked over the empty square.

"I'll see you next Saturday." She called back.

"Next Saturday." Mathilda replied

Claudia looked up and there was her mother.

"Claudia Ding, will you answer me?" she was saying

"Sorry Mum."

"I'll say again, is there anything you need while we are in town."
"No I don't think so. I've got everything I was hoping for today."

Chapter 4 Swinegate

"You have a plan then?"

"Yes. A plan that is impossible to fail."

"It had better not."
"I assure you it won't."

"I shall trust you this once but if you let me down there will be consequences."

*

The next few Saturdays were amongst the happiest days of Claudia's young life as she and Mathilda explored this new version of York that was so familiar and yet so different. She'd get the bus into town with her mother, get through all of the boring tasks like the bank, library and piano before finally getting to Kings Square to meet with Mathilda and off they'd go exploring.

The street layout of the city was exactly the same as the one she was used to and many of the buildings and decorations in the city were exactly the same as in her old world. But then some things would appear where she had never seen them before. Viking houses along Coppergate, Victorian gas works in Hungate and a several medieval churches that she could swear hadn't been there last time she looked. Mathilda explained that these were all echoes of structures that had been there once, even if they had long been swept away and replaced with new buildings in the name of progress.

People could leave an echo as well, Mathilda went on, maybe not directly and maybe the echo they leave behind is distorted quite considerably from the original person but an echo would be there none the less. There were also those who lived just in the Echo World. People like Gus and Meg who have only known one world. Claudia was interested in everyone that she met of course but she was mostly interested in just how few people there were on the streets. In her version of York she could sometimes barely move amongst all the shoppers, tourists and tour guides moving their way around the streets. In this world she had space and time to move around and view everything in her own way. Going into the city centre no longer felt like a chore, it felt like a treat.

"SWINE"

The cry took Claudia by complete surprise as they were happily walking down the street

"Swine. Swine's-a-coming."

Mathilda grabbed Claudia's hand and ushered them down a side alleyway.

"We'll be safe down here" She assured Claudia.

The first thing she heard were the feint sounds of footsteps in the distance. Quickly the sound grew and grew into a thunder of trotters hitting pavement interspersed with the squeals of pigs.

"Now you'll see why this street is called Swinegate!" Mathilda said to her.

Claudia thought back to something her mother had told her about this street getting its name by once being the home of York's pig market. Not that she was interested in anything her mother told her.

Then the animals started rushing past them. First came their piglets, running as fast as their little legs could carry them, their high pitched squeals piercing Claudia's ears. Then came the full grown pigs, their heavier feet hitting the pavement hard and loud and making lower but equally deafening noises. Finally came the wild boars, massive beasts with fierce looking tusks. There weren't squealing like small ones but grunting and snorting at a fearsome volume.

After the last boar had passed them, Claudia turned to Mathilda and they poked their heads out of the snickleway.

All of the swine had reached the end of Swinegate and had turned left onto Church Street but Claudia was amazed to find that as they disappeared from round the corner, the sound diminished very quickly. By the time that the last pig went out of view, there was no sound of them at all. In fact, there was no evidence that they had been there at all.

"Where do they go?" Claudia asked

"Nobody knows." Mathilda answered vaguely. "They just appear every now and then and only when someone is down on Swinegate. No one has ever seen them from Church Street or any other direction."

"So we just have to jump down a snickleway and hope for the best?"

"Pretty much yes. This alley is always a good one to hide in. It's called Mad Alice Lane but don't worry, once you get to know Alice you realise that stories about her are vastly exaggerated."

*

"Pie Iesu Domine, dona eis requiem."

The slow rhythmic chanting grew in volume as it came towards them. Claudia was sure it was medieval monks.

"Pie Iesu Domine, dona eis requiem."

She saw the monks now, each one dressed entirely in black with long robes and black hoods pulled up over their heads so that no one could see any of their faces.

"Pie Iesu Domine, dona eis requiem."

Over and over, the same chant. Or maybe it was best to describe it as a song. They were all in unison, all with the same rhythm, all stretching out the last word as long as they could.

"We call them the Blackfriars." Mathilda could see Claudia watching and puzzling over the chanters. "They move around the city, marching and chanting in unison. They don't cause any harm."

"How long have they been here?" Claudia asked.

"As long as anybody can remember. There are a few groups of them around the city. There's the Blackfriars here but also the Greyfriars and Whitefriars. You'll get used to figuring out which is which from what they are chanting. All in Latin of course but all different."

As the Blackfriars walked off into the distance Claudia and Mathilda continued their walk through the city. They walked up The Shambles waving a brief hello to Gus and Meg, up Swinegate hoping to avoid any stampedes then past the medieval Barley Hall before turning right onto Stonegate. As they went through the city, Mathilda explained about York's history. Unlike when her mother bored her death, Claudia did not mind it when Mathilda talked about these things. In fact she found it fascinating.

"Stonegate is a street that many visitors to York have mistaken for the more famous Shambles. It also has the same style of overhanging timber framed and plaster medieval buildings with their upper stories sticking out over street level. However compared to The Shambles, Stonegate is a considerably longer and wider street. It was originally laid as a Roman road called the Via Praetoria and the modern name Stonegate is actually over 1,000 years old. It's a Viking word meaning A Street with Stones. It's not a very imaginative name but one that does a job. Mind you, it's a bit more imaginative that calling a street Pavement just because it is the first street in the city with pavement. In the middle ages, Stonegate was the big shopping street in York and people came to buy expensive clothing, they came to buy jewellery and they came to get drunk. Nowadays however, people come here to buy expensive clothing, come here to buy jewellery or come here to get drunk. So things don't really change do they?"

"Hellooooo."

The long drawn greeting stopped them in their tracks. Claudia looked around but couldn't see anybody who might be talking to them.

"Hellooooo."

It came again. She looked around again but still couldn't see anybody on the street. It was only when she looked up that she found who was speaking. Above a doorway was a small stone cat. He was carefully stretching out his front legs and arching his back as if waking from a long sleep. Claudia had seen the cat before when she and her Mother had done the cat trail but she was sure he wasn't moving then. And he was definitely not speaking when she saw him before.

"Hello." Claudia replied nervously.

"It's good to see you." The cat continued, purring as he spoke.

"It's...erm...good to see you as well."

Claudia looked at Mathilda with a smile. Mathilda didn't seem that surprised to see a talking statue. Not even a talking statue of a cat. The stone cat jumped down to street level, expertly using the door frames and window ledges to get down quickly and safely. Still purring he began rubbing against Claudia's legs, she bent down to stroke him but the cat jumped backwards out of her reach.

"I never said you could touch me" he said defensively, looking up at her with a shocked look.

Claudia couldn't help laughing. Gently she put her hand close, but not too close, to the cat. Carefully, the cat sniffed her hand, thought about things for a couple of seconds and then began brushing his head against her hand and purring loudly. Claudia laughed again.

"What's so funny?" The cat asked through the purrs.

"It's just the way you came up to me, rubbing against me like I was your best friend in the world and then complained when I tried to stroke you." She replied.

"I just wanted to do things in my own time." The Stonecat sounded just as self-important as Claudia always imagined cats would sound.

"What about what we wanted to do?" Mathilda asked with a mischievous grin.

"As I cat, I don't worry too much about what other people want." Stonecat said dismissively "As long as I'm happy then that's all I'm interested in."

"Do you know the other cats in York?" Claudia asked

"Other cats? Yes, I know them but I don't have anything to do with them." The cat shot a jealous look over towards Claudia "Why, which other cats have you met?"

"The two black cats in St Andrewgate."

"Oh those two idiots. Always fighting, you'd never catch me doing that. Any others?"

"The wool cat on The Shambles."

"Oh that idiot, always collapsing into a ball of wool. And as for the one on the pub roof in Kings Square, he's the biggest idiot of the lot. He's been stalking that same bird for years and still hasn't worked out that it is just a statue."

"Surely if the bird is just a statue then the cat must be a statue as well?" Claudia sounded confused.

The cat jumped back from her in shock.

"We cats are not statues." He said, clearly taking great offence at her words. "We just like to sleep a lot. And when we are moving most people don't look carefully enough to see us."

Having overcome his disgust with her, Stonecat came back close up to Claudia and rubbed his face on her fingers, clearly expecting her to tickle him under his chin. Being made out of stone he definitely wasn't as soft and furry as other cats she had known but she found herself tickling him anyway. The cat responded by throwing his head back, closing his eyes and purring like a train. Despite the fact that the cat was selfish and dismissive of others, Claudia couldn't help but find him funny and adorable.

"Sorry Stonecat, we'd love to stay here with you." Mathilda said "But we've got to be moving along."

"Oh yes, well I can't stay here any longer either." Stonecat replied, desperate to make it appear that he was the one making all of the decisions.

With a few leaps and bounds the cat was back above the doorway. He went around in circles for a few seconds, sniffing the ground as he went before settling down and appearing to go to sleep. Only a quick glimpse towards Claudia through one briefly opened eye gave the game away.

What a strange and wonderful world this was. Claudia knew that she and Mathilda would have so much fun here for a long, long time.

*

And then one Saturday Mathilda wasn't there. Claudia tried not to be upset and told herself that it would have been selfish of her to assume that Mathilda would give up every Saturday just to show someone around.

But there was no sign of Mathilda the following week either. Or the week after, or the week after that. Claudia was confused, she thought she had made a close friend and couldn't understand why Mathilda would just disappear without a trace. She began to wonder again whether she had imagined the whole thing. Maybe her Saturdays were going to go back to boring history lectures, piano lessons and shopping. How disappointing.

Until she stepped off the 415 bus one Saturday and a man thrust a piece of paper towards her. She took the paper by instinct without getting a good look at the man. She looked up towards her mother to see her reaction but her mother wasn't there. In fact she realised that there was no one around her. All of the people who had just been standing there had simply disappeared. Claudia knew immediately that she was in the Echo World.

Realising the paper must be significant, she nervously opened it up and found writing on the inside.

Claudia,

I hope you get this. I need your help. The Queen of Shadows has captured me. Look for me Claudia, I need you. Look for the Peterkeys, stop her finding them. Look for Balthazar, he will help you.

You'll find me, I know you will

Mathilda

Chapter 5 The Stonebow

"You'll never get away with this."

"Oh but we already have."

*

Claudia was stunned. Mathilda had been taken? When was she taken? Where was she? Who was The Queen of Shadows? Who was Balthazar? What were the Peterkeys?

Then she remembered she knew the answer to one of those questions. Balthazar was the wise looking old man in the long white robes that she thought she might have offended when they first met. She hadn't seen him at all since then but he had seemed intelligent and thoughtful man. If Mathilda thought he was the right man to help then he must be the right man to help. He had said that he could always be found on the corner of The Stonebow and Fossgate so that was a good place to start looking. But first she needed time to think. She decided to visit Gus and Meg.

"Claudia, we've been worried about you. Where have you been?" Meg called out.

"Hello Meg." Claudia replied.

"Why haven't you been coming to see us? And where's Mathilda?"

"I don't know. I've not seen Mathilda in a few weeks. One Saturday she just didn't show up. That's when I stopped coming to your world."

"Oh...Gus, did you hear that?" Meg called into the back of the shop.

"Claudia hasn't seen Mathilda either."

"Oh, that's odd." Gus came to the front of the shop with a concerned look on his face. "We've been worried about her for a while but thought she was busy with you."

Claudia considered showing Gus and Meg the note. They were obviously concerned about Mathilda and would be sure to help her if she asked. But the note only said to find Balthazar and didn't mention anyone else so Claudia decided that she was going to go straight to see him. Besides, she tried to convince herself, telling them would only cause them worry.

Claudia wanted to move on quickly but didn't want to seem rude so allowed herself to stay for a small chat and even smaller slice of Victoria sponge, just to be polite of course. Afterwards she bid her goodbyes with Gus and Meg keen to stress that Claudia should come and see them anytime and let them know as soon as she had found anything about Mathilda.

Claudia walked nervously down the rest of The Shambles towards where she had last seen Balthazar.

Then all of a sudden the fog was everywhere. It had come down so fast that Claudia was sure that something terrible had happened. One minute she was walking happily along without a care in the world and the next minute she couldn't see more than a metre ahead of her. And there was near silence. No noises from her own world, no noises from the echo world. There just seemed to be nothing and nobody around her. The only sound she could now hear was a faint droning noise. At first it was barely noticeable, just a low hum in the far distance. But the sound was building, building, getting louder every second. Then through the fog she saw the outline of a figure, it was very difficult to see exactly who it was but she thought it was a man. Slowly the figure became clearer through the mist, Claudia began to make out a young man with dark hair, a small moustache under his nose and wearing a military uniform. She recognised the uniform from a school project she had done on the 2nd World War and could tell that the man was a fighter pilot. That would make sense, if he was a pilot then the drone she could hear would be planes flying towards them.

Claudia and the pilot looked at each for a moment. The sound of planes almost directly overhead, although she had no way of seeing through the fog exactly where they were. The pilot was the first to speak.

"Hello" He said quietly.

"Hello" Claudia replied nervously.

"Don't be scared of the fog." The pilot seemed to be able to read Claudia's mind.

"I'm not scared." She tried her best to sound confident "I'm just not sure what's happening. I don't like not being able to see the way."

"Don't be afraid. In life you can't always see where you are going. Sometimes the fog gets too thick. It's nothing to fear."

The man spoke with a foreign accent. Claudia could not tell where he was from.

 "What is your name?" He asked her

"Claudia. What's your name?"

"Yves."

"Eve. Like E-V-E."

"Well my name is pronounced like that but it is spelled Y-V-E-S."

"Oh. Is that a foreign name?"

"Yes. I am French."

She had a thought.

"What language are you speaking?" She asked.

"French"

"Oh"

"Why" he asked in return "What language are you speaking"

"English"

"Oh."

Whatever languages they were speaking they understood each perfectly well. Claudia looked at the man, the fact that he was still dressed in his pilot's uniform seemed significant.

"Did you fight in the war?" She asked.

Yves thought long and hard for a second.

"I think I did yes." He eventually said uncertainly.

"Were you a pilot?"

Again the man thought long and hard. The memory was clearly hard to come by.

"That's right, I was a pilot yes."

"What are you doing in this world?"

"I'm not sure. Maybe I'm just a shadow or an echo from another world."

The two looked at each other again. Yves closed his eyes and began to disappear back into the thickening mist.

"Don't be afraid of the fog Claudia." He said as vanished from view.

And with that she was back where she had been before. No fog, no sound of aeroplanes overhead, just her making her way towards The Stonebow where she hoped to find Balthazar.

There was no one around when Claudia got there. What had Balthazar said, look for him there and she could always find him. Well there was no sign of him at all. This wasn't a very good start.

She took a good look around and oh, there he was. Standing around casually as if he had always been there.

"Hello there." Balthazar said to her in his calm manner "You are Mathilda's young friend aren't you. Claudia isn't it? Have you come to look me?"
"Yes I am, I was hoping you could help me."

Claudia explained about how Mathilda had disappeared and how the man the given her the note. She gave the note to Balthazar and he read it slowly and carefully without a hint of emotion.

"So why did Mathilda tell me to find you." Claudia asked.

"I'm not sure." He answered.

"Do you know her well?"

"Not really."

"Oh." Claudia couldn't help but sound dejected. "What about the rest of the note?"

"The Queen of Shadows means nothing to me."

This was not going as well as Claudia had hoped it would.

"But the Peterkeys, yes I know about the Peterkeys." Balthazar continued.

Finally, things were sounding positive.

"So where can I find them?" Claudia asked.

"I don't know, they are scattered somewhere around the city. No one knows where they've been hidden."

The look of confusion and disappointment must have been very evident of Claudia's face as Balthazar took a deep breath and began explaining.

"Maybe I should start at the beginning." He said carefully "As you know, York is surrounded by its city walls. They were built to stop anyone getting in and out of the city without permission. There were four major entrances through the walls."

"Yes I remember. They are called the Bars aren't they? My mother says that soldiers used to be in there stopping people getting in and that the gates be locked every night." Claudia was pleased with herself for remembering.

"That is exactly right. Micklegate Bar, Bootham Bar, Walmgate Bar and Monk Bar. Each one is a 4 story fortress in its own right. Each one with its own set of heavy doorways and iron portcullis to stop anyone getting through it. At one point in the Echo World they were locked permanently using what were called the Peterkeys."

"Why were they locked?"

"Some people believed that the echoes of York needed to stay inside they city. They worried that if they were allowed to escape then they would become diluted and weakened. But others thought that the echoes should be allowed to escape the city so that people from outside of York can learn about our history and come into the city to benefit from all of the wonderful things that York has to offer."

"So what happened?"

"Many years ago, those that believed in letting the echoes out won the argument. As such it was decided that the gates were going to be opened permanently and so the Peterkeys were hidden around the city to stop anybody using them. My guess is that someone, this Queen of Shadows has started looking for the keys so that she can control the gateways and control the passage of echoes in and out of the city.

"Ok, but surely nowadays there are no longer only four ways through the walls. There are loads of archways and gaps in the walls that have been added so that people can walk and drive through them."

"Yes but once all the gates are locked with the Peterkeys, and only with the Peterkeys, then all of these gaps and archways will no longer exist and the walls will once again be the defensive structures that they were when they were first built."

Claudia thought hard for a moment. This seemed serious. Whoever this Queen of Shadows was she seemed to be messing with something important. Plus, she had captured Claudia's friend and so needed stopping quickly. She needed to get to work straight away.

"So where do I start looking for the Peterkeys?" She asked determinedly.

"I'm afraid I can't help you there." Balthazar replied "But if you are half as observant as I think you are then I'm sure you'd be exactly the person who can find them. And if you ever need my help, you know where to find me."

"Thank you Balthazar, you've been most helpful."

Claudia smiled nervously at Balthazar and turned to walk away. Her mind was racing with all this talk of keys and walls and bars. All she wanted to do was get back to her mother and her own world to try and make sense of things.

"Oh and Claudia." Balthazar called out to her "This could be very dangerous. Someone's already captured Mathilda and could be trying to hurt you. Don't trust anybody. Don't trust a single person, not even the people that you like most in this world."

Chapter 6 Museum Street

We are all able to hear the echoes, we all create new echoes, we are the echoes of York.

*

Claudia had spent almost the entire hour of her mother's history lesson searching the library for anything to do with the Peterkeys. She'd come up with precisely nothing and had come to the conclusion that the keys were only things that existed in Mathilda's world. She had hoped that there would be some sort of echo of them in her own but it appeared not to be the case.

She was frustrated and disappointed. She needed some time to be by herself. She was still getting used to going into the Echo World by herself so maybe this was a good time to try it out. She went to the front door of the library, watched the people coming in and out and listened to the noise of traffic of Museum Street bustled past outside. She took a deep breath, closed her eyes and stepped through the door. Slowly she opened her eyes again in the hope that she had made it through to the other world. Sure enough the traffic was gone, there was nobody on the streets, and she had made it to the other world. Claudia couldn't help but feel a little pleased with herself.

It was all quiet and peaceful outside, just a gentle tap-tap-tap from around the corner. Claudia took another deep breath, determined to enjoy this moment of tranquillity without getting distracted. Tap-tap-tap. Yes there was no chance of her getting distracted by anything. Tap-tap-

tap. Right that did it, she was going to find out where that noise was coming from.

She walked around the corner of the building towards the stretch of the city walls that could be found next to the library. To her surprise, there was a group of three men working on top of the city walls. They appeared to actually be building and the tap-tap-tap was the sound of hammer and chisels as they shaped the stones. Claudia thought hard back to what her mother had told her, this stretch of the city walls were the oldest of the entire city. In fact, weren't they built by the Romans? The men working on the wall were dressed the same as the Roman soldiers she had seen in Kings Square. However, unlike in Kings Square, this stretch of Roman wall was still standing in Claudia's own world. Admittedly there wasn't usually Roman Legionaries on top of them but none the less they were still there to be admired and marvelled at.

"Hello there." One of the legionaries called towards her "Can we help?"

They could see her as well. That was a surprise. Claudia realised that she must have been quite blatantly staring directly at them. She felt very rude but then it wasn't every day that you saw 2000 year old echoes in front of your face.

"Hello." She called back hesitantly "I didn't mean to disturb you."

"That's OK. I could do with a break anyway." The Legionary called back.

"We're getting a break?" One of the other Legionaries cried out in excitement.

"Fantastic. I'm absolutely shattered." The third called out putting down his hammer.

"Not you two." The first declared with some authority. *"I'm* getting a break to talk to our young guest. You two are going to keep building. So keep building."

The two obviously lower ranked Legionaries begrudgingly took up their tools again and gave their superior a dirty look.

Tap-tap-tap

They began again.

"My name is Lucius Duccius Rufinus." The Legionary declared with some pride "I am Standard Bearer for the Legion based here in York."

"Pleased to meet you Lush Ducky Rough Ness." Claudia knew she wasn't saying his name right. She hoped he didn't mind. After all he was a rather big man. And he had armour. And a sword.

"That's OK, you can stick with calling me Rufinus. Can you say that?" He said gently

"Roo- fine –us." Claudia repeated carefully.

"We get used to people not being able to speak Latin. We've had plenty of practice over the years. This here is Augustinus and over there is Diogenes." Rufinus pointed at his fellow Legionaries.

"Nice to meet all of you. My name is Claudia Ding."

The three of them nodded politely in her direction.

"How long have you been building this wall?" Claudia asked.

"Too long." Augustinus replied

"Far too long." Diogenes backed up his friend whilst being careful not to look up from his work in case he got told off. As it happened, Rufinus appeared to agree

"Oh yes we've been building this wall for a long, long time. We've seen the city change over and over in that time. People come and people go, the city grows and shrinks and grows again. Sometimes you can barely see for people crushing into the city looking for jobs and money, sometimes it's much quieter. But it's always York. It's always this place of history and magic. It's always...."

"Cold."
"Augustinus. Do not interrupt me. It's always....well it is always cold I guess."
"And wet" Diogenes joined in.

"Well yes it is cold and wet. Especially compared from where we came from."
"Did you come from Rome?"

"Not exactly no. The Roman Empire covered the entire area of Europe and beyond. I'm actually from what you'd now call France. Wonderful place it was, I was so happy there. " Rufinus spoke with a faraway look in his eyes. "When I joined the army I had no idea I was going to get sent out here to the absolute furthest north I could go."

"It's the clouds that get me." Augustinus was not even pretending to work anymore "And the fog. Especially this time of year now that we are firmly into autumn. I'm from Spain, a land when the sun shines all the time. As far as I remember anyway. My wife, Flavia Augustina, says that she actually likes it here. She says that she doesn't have to worry so much about getting burnt by the sun or it being too hot to work. She even says that the rain and cloud gives the place a really lush green look and that the fog gives the place a sense of mystery. But not me, no I miss the sun."

"My wife, Julia Fortunata doesn't like it here." Diogenes said wistfully. "As she tells me all too regularly."

"Where do you come from?" Claudia asked.

"Sardinia. Have you ever been?"

"No I haven't. What's it like?"

"Oh it's a wonderful place. It's an island in the Mediterranean Sea. It's warm and calm, filled with hills and forests. There are rocky cliffs and sandy beaches. Julia Fortunata begs that someday she'll get to go back there."

The three men were now all lost in their own thoughts. Happy in their memories exploring the far off places that they had long left behind.

"Right enough of this." Rufinus eventually snapped his comrades out of their daydreaming "This wall won't build itself."

They got back to work.

Tap-tap-tap went the hammer and chisel.

Tap-tap-tap.

Tap-tap-tap.

It was almost musical the way they hammered to a rhythm

Tap-tap-tap.

Tap-tap-tap.

Claudia realised it was more musical than she thought as the men had started singing. All singing along to the rhythm of the hammers

We came from far off countries.

No strangers to the sun

We saw the British weather

And wondered what we'd done

So we toil away

In fog and wind and rain

The Legate always tells us

Bring peace unto the region

And no one does it better

Than the victorious 6th Legion

And we'll never tire

The Roman Legion Choir

We know we'll get the orders

We know we'll get the call

The Emperor will tell us

To build another wall

We'll build higher and higher

The Roman Legion Choir

And we'll never tire

The Roman Legion Choir

Claudia felt reassured. No matter what happened, no matter the bad things that she was experiencing, life would go on as ever. The same life that had been in this city for 2,000 years would still go on and keep on leaving its echoes. People would come and go but this would always be York. The wonderful, magical place of York.

Claudia felt it was the right time to return to the library. Maybe if she looked inside now there would be different books and she might find something about the Peterkeys. She said her goodbyes to her new friends and set off back around the corner.

She walked into the building with a contented smile on her face, with nobody else in there she could hear her own steps echoing as she walked up the stairs to the local history section. Claudia wondered if she would leave a permanent echo in the city like those Roman Soldiers had done. Whoever Yves the Airman was he had also done something to leave a permanent echo here as well. What does it take to leave a trace of yourself for future generations?

Claudia was lost in her own thoughts when she heard a noise. She stopped what she was doing and listened, it sounded like footsteps. She wasn't alone in here. She began to panic, if she wasn't alone maybe she was in danger. Balthazar had warned her that someone might be out to get her. The footsteps got closer, whoever it was coming her way. Claudia felt herself shrinking against the shelves in an attempt to go unnoticed. After what seemed like hours a figure finally came into view and looked at her

"Hello Claudia. I thought I'd find you here."

"Lucy Cavendish, what are you doing in the Echo World?"

Lucy was stood in front of her larger than life and as happy as ever.

"You're from this world as well?" Claudia asked.

"Well I can go in between the worlds. Nowadays I spend most of my time in your world because I enjoy working in a busy library but I'm from the echo world originally. There aren't many of us so welcome to the exclusive club."

"How did you know I'd be able to come here?"

"Over the years I've met a few other people who could travel between the worlds. You get good at picking out who can do it. It's usually those people who are best at watching, listening and seeing things that other people miss. Sometimes the ability to go between worlds runs in families, sometimes not."

"So what happens to all of these people?"

"Often the first time they go into the echo world they panic and convince themselves it was all in their imagination and never come back again. Sometimes they find themselves living entirely in one world and forget that they had never been to the other world. Hopefully you'll be one of those people who never stops being able to go between the worlds."

"So is this place a library in both worlds?" Claudia asked

"It is indeed. As you can see it is never as busy as in your world but people still use it as a library."

"Are the books in here the same in both worlds?"

"Some are the same. Some are different. Was there any particular book you were looking for?"

Claudia remembered Balthazar's advice not to trust anybody and decided not let Lucy know what she doing.

"Nothing really no." Claudia said trying to act cool "I guess if there was a general book covering the history of the Echo World. Just so that I can get to grips on how this world differs from mine."

"But how would you know the difference?" Lucy asked with a twinkle in her eye "When you take so little interest in the local history of your own city."

Claudia shuffled with embarrassment. "Well...erm...I don't...I guess..."

"OK don't worry, I'm just teasing. Wellbeloved's is always a good place to start. Now where is it?" Lucy started searching through a shelf of books before pulling one out triumphantly. "Here it is. This is a great introduction our version of York. And he would help a lot with understanding your own world."

Claudia looked at the front of the cover of the book that Lucy had handed to her. *Charles Wellbeloved's Encyclopaedia of All Things York.* Well that seemed just about perfect.

"Can I borrow this book?" She asked.

"Well this is a library. Lending books is something that we occasionally do."

"Thank you for that. I might have a look through it now if that is OK. Thanks again Lucy, I'm glad to see you here."

"And you Claudia. This really has made my day."

Chapter 7 Baille Hill

"York was founded by the Romans in 71 AD. They were attracted by flat, fertile farmland surrounded by a horseshoe of beautiful, resource rich hills. Most importantly, they were attracted by the amazing network of interconnected rivers that brought York in easy contact with the hills, the farmland and out to the high seas. Originally, this was a place of soldiers, strong defences and stone walls but soon it became a city of trade, wealth and place for people from all across the Empire to come calling. Emperors themselves came to visit.

The Romans were here for over 300 years and even centuries later Saints, Popes and Kings knew that controlling York meant controlling the North of England. The Anglo-Saxons made this place the mother church and a great seat of learning. When the most powerful man in Europe needed someone to run his schools, there was only one place to look for him and that was in York.

It's no wonder that when the Vikings were determined to violently bring this place under their rule. Despite their bloodthirsty reputation and their fearsomely named rulers, the Vikings also brought industry, wealth and luxury goods that had travelled thousands of miles to get here. During this time the city expanded and more defences were put up to keep the city enclosed and safe.

By the time William the Conqueror got here, York had been a thriving, bustling place for 1000 years. Yet there was still more building to be done; houses, halls, castles and walls all became larger than ever before. And of course The Minster kept on growing and growing until it became the biggest and grandest building around. The medieval city was stuffed to the gills with bishops and monks, adventurous merchants and busy workers, Kings and Queens and Dukes and Earls.

Even when other cities began to grow larger than York in the Industrial Revolution, you could still come here to find factories, railways, shops, restaurants, schools, universities and museums.

All these people, all this life and all this history were crammed into an area of just half a square mile. Each event, each vibration causing echoes that bounced around the inside of the mighty stone walls are still here for everyone to find if they just look for them. Although you may never meet the people who created the echo, you still get to walk down the streets they walked down, go into the buildings that they built, look at the things that they made. Every time a historian finds something new, every time a child reads a story, every time a visitor to the city gawps in wonder at a beautiful building, they are hearing the echo of someone who lived here many years before them. And new echoes are constantly being made by the most recent souls to inhabit this area. We are all able to hear the echoes, we all create new echoes, we are the echoes of York."

Charles Wellbeloved's Encyclopaedia of All Things York, Page 1

*

Claudia couldn't wait to have a search through this new book and find all the references to the Peterkeys. She turned to the index at the back of the book and began looking through the P's for any mention of the Peterkeys. There was nothing there.

Maybe they were under K for key? No, nothing there either.

She looked through the book for all of the references for the City Walls and the Bars. She read once again the story that Balthazar had told her about the argument about whether the gates should be locked or kept open but she found absolutely no reference at all to any keys or where they might be hidden.

Claudia was frustrated. She wondered if she would ever find anything out about these flipping keys. She began flicking through the book for anything that might help her at all when something caught her attention. She recognised immediately that it was a map of the city centre of York. The shape of the medieval city was determined by the walls that enclosed them and these were picked out on the map in thick black lines. All the important landmarks of the city such as The Minster and the castle were displayed prominently as well as the major streets such as Parliament Street, Stonegate and The Shambles. She searched around the map and was intrigued to see that the four Bars had all been displayed in different colours. The medieval gateway called Micklegate Bar on the west side of the city was coloured red, the gateway on the far south-east of the city called Walmgate Bar was coloured silver and the gateways on the north side of the city called Monk Bar and Bootham Bar were coloured blue and gold respectively.

There was something else that had taken Claudia's attention. In the top right hand corner of the page there was a key, not a key to a door unfortunately but the type of keys that maps had to help you understand what you were looking. This key however was different to any other that Claudia had seen, there was just four lines of writing, each in a different colour.

In red were written the words "Perhaps buried in the castle too."

In silver were the words "A sharp key, maybe too sharp or alternatively it may be flat."

In blue the words "For a wild test, eat thirty."

And in gold the words "Part of the last will. I am sure you will find what you seek if you ask politely."

None of the sentences made any sense at all. She knew where the castle was but not what was buried there. "Alternatively it may be flat", "Part of the last will." It was all utter gibberish. Eat thirty what? Claudia felt that she could eat thirty raisins easily enough or maybe thirty strawberries or if she really, really had to she could eat thirty pieces of chocolate but if the test was to eat thirty turnips then she might struggle. And yet...and yet it must be related to what she was searching for. There were four bars; one red, one silver, one blue and one gold. There were four lines of writing in the key; one red, one silver, one blue and one gold. It was far too much of a coincidence.

"You look deep in thought, what have you found there?"

Claudia was deep in thought, so deep in fact that she hadn't noticed Lucy Cavendish sneak up on her. Claudia was still wary about trusting anybody with her important task and considered slamming the book shut. On the other hand Lucy probably wasn't sneaking anywhere and besides trying to hide what she was reading would only look suspicious.

"Nothing important." She said with a nervous smile "Just a map of York, I was just interested in this key here and what all this writing meant"

"Can I have a look……oh yes, I've seen this map in Wellbeloved before but I have to admit that I never understood what it was all about. It's all a bit confusing really. What are you meant to eat thirty of? I've always hoped that the test was to eat thirty biscuits."

"So you haven't any idea about it at all."

"Not really no. Except that it all sounds a bit like a cryptic clues. There must ways of deciphering each clue but I have no idea what."

"So what sort of things are in cryptic clues?"

"Well it's always been a bit of a mystery to me. Lots of words that can have double meanings and lots of anagrams. Do you know about anagrams?"

"Are they when you change the orders of the letters in one word to make another?"

"That's right yes, so Melon is an anagram of Lemon or Astronomer is an anagram of Moon Starer."

There was a silence as both Lucy and Claudia thought about what had been said and how they could decipher the key in the map.

"Oh well, it's something to keep me busy isn't it." Claudia eventually said, trying to play it cool.

"Yes indeed. And if you do ever figure it out and of the clues then come and let me know."

*

Claudia couldn't stop thinking about the map she had found and the strange, cryptic messages that were written in the key. She had spoken to Balthazar about it and although he was delighted that she had found something that looked important he had no idea how to decipher the messages. In the end, she swallowed her pride and did something she thought she would never do.

"Mum, what's buried at the castle?" she asked her mother.

The red clue, "Perhaps buried at the castle too" seemed like the clue that her mother would be most likely to help her with. If she was right, solving this clue would give her the location of the Peterkey for Micklegate Bar, as this was also coloured red on the map.

"What's buried at the castle?" Her mother repeated with a confused look on her face. "I'm not too sure what you mean. And what's brought on this sudden interest in the castle?"

"Oh nothing really. Just something I read at the library."
"Ok dear, well I'm always happy to talk about history."

"Great." Claudia knew all too well how happy her mother was to talk about history. And talk, and talk and talk about history. However, she decided to press on "York Castle is now called Clifford's Tower isn't it?"

"Absolutely correct honey. Actually the tower is the only remaining part of what would have been a much bigger medieval castle. Most of the buildings were pulled down in the 18th Century and the castle area was turned into a prison. Do you remember we've visited the old prison cells, they're now part of York Castle Museum? You always used to be so scared of going down into them without someone holding your hand."

"They were really creepy." Claudia replied suddenly realising just how terrified she used to be of the old prison cells.

Claudia's mother took a deep breath and Claudia felt a lecture coming on. She settled in for the long haul as her mother continued.

"Originally it was built as a motte and bailey castle. That's when you pile up a mound of earth and put a tower on top of it which is called a motte and then build a load of other buildings at the base of the mound that is called the bailey. In 1080 William the Conqueror ordered two motte and bailey castles built in York, one either side of the river. They were an important part of medieval life...."

The lecture had begun. Claudia let her mother speak on and allowed her own thoughts to drift off onto other things. It was a tried and trusted technique she had often employed whenever she was didn't want to listen. Although....hang on.

"Wow." She loudly interrupted her mother's lecture "Did you say there were two castles?"

"Yes that's right. There was the building that's now called Clifford's Tower on this side of the river and another castle on the other side of the river."

"So what happened to the other castle?

"Well, after a while people stopped using it and all of the walls were taken down so the castle isn't there anymore. The mound of earth that it was built on is still there though. The mound is now called Baille Hill."

Claudia knew where Baille Hill was, she just never knew it was originally a castle. Or at least, she had never listened to her mother when she'd been repeatedly told that it was a castle.

"So you could call Baille Hill York's castle two. Castle number two I mean." Claudia asked

"I guess you could yes. I don't think anyone ever has done but if you wanted to you could call Baille Hill York's castle two."

*

"I've found one of the keys." Claudia bounded up to Balthazar full of excitement and enthusiasm. She had been so keen to get to Balthazar that she had simply abandoned her mother mid lecture and gone straight in to the Echo World.

"You've found one, that's fantastic. Where was it?" Balthazar replied with as much emotion as Claudia felt he was capable of achieving. Which really wasn't much.

"Well, I say I've found the key. I haven't actually found it but what I actually mean is I think I know where the key is." Claudia was backtracking massively on her earlier promise.

"OK. So which key do you think you've found?"

"The red key. The clue says that it is buried in the castle too. Except that, it doesn't mean it is buried in the castle as well, it means that it is buried in castle number two."

"And where is castle number two?"
"Baille Hill."

"Of course, Baille Hill. It sounds obvious now you say it. I'd entirely forgotten that used to be a castle."

Claudia felt proud. Now all she needed to do was a way to find the key itself. It could be buried anywhere in the hill and she didn't want to have to spend hours desperately digging in the hope of finding it.

"You should go to North Street Gardens." Balthazar continued "I don't think that Mathilda ever took you there but in the gardens you'll find a man called Neville. He will be able to help you find the key."

Chapter 8 Skeldergate

"According to the Viking Sagas, a fearsome warlord named Ragnar Lodbrok (which translates into English as Ragnar Hairy Trousers) terrorised York and the North East England in the mid-9th century. However, Ragnar's reign of terror was brought to an abrupt end when he was captured and killed in York by being thrown into a pit of poisonous snakes. The sagas go on to say that Ragnar was avenged by his sons Ivar the Boneless, Halfdan the Black and Ubba when they in turn captured York, took their father's killer prisoner and brutally murdered him. How much of the stories in the sagas are true is unknown but whatever the truth the biggest mystery of all remains where they would have got poisonous snakes in Yorkshire."

Charles Wellbeloved's Encyclopaedia of All Things York, Page 87

*

Claudia was excited to go in search of the man called Neville who might help her find the red key. Using the map in Wellbeloved's Encyclopaedia as her guide, she left Balthazar and headed along Pavement and Coppergate before crossing the river over Ouse Bridge and turning right on her way to North Street Gardens.

The gardens themselves were not big. Maybe 20 metres long and 10 metres wide with some seating amongst the flowerbeds so that people could enjoy the views of the river. As she got to the gardens she noticed a man on his knees and tending to the plants in one of the flowerbeds. Was this the man called Neville that she was searching for?

"Hello." She said to the man "They're nice flowers."

"Roses." The man replied curtly

"I'm sorry?" Claudia asked in confusion

"Oh no need to apologise. I forgive you."

"Right. Sorry...erm... no, not sorry...erm...I'm not sure what's going on."

"Roses. They are nice roses."

"Sorry. They are nice roses." Claudia didn't want to keep on apologising but couldn't stop herself.

"Red roses. They are nice red roses." The man was still as curt as ever.

"Yes, nice red roses. Sorry again."

"As I say, no need to apologise. I forgive you."

This was not going very well. If this was the man that she needed to help her then everything was going to be much harder than she thought. She gave the man a good look over, he was a fairly short man with shoulder length hair and a neat beard. He wore a brightly coloured tunic, mostly yellow but decorated with blue lions. He looked intense and brooding, as if totally dedicated to his task.

"Are you responsible for all of these flowers?" Claudia tried again to get him onside while gesturing to the plants around her.

"I grow the red roses. I only grow red roses. If you want anything else grown here then that's entirely up to you."

The man had not looked up from his beloved roses during the entire conversation. Red roses as he kept on insisting on telling her, which Claudia thought was odd because she thought that York always had white roses. Yet another thing she didn't quite understand. Maybe a different approach was required.

"I'm looking for a man named Neville." She asked directly "Do you know him?"

The man carefully placed his gardening tools on the ground, took a deep breath and looked up at Claudia.

"Please don't mentioned that name." He said with a serious look on his face.

The man stood up and walked over towards an old fashioned, hand operated water pump. He picked up a watering can and began pumping water into the can. Claudia was not sure what to do next. Whoever this man was, he clearly wasn't going to help her find Neville.

"No no no. No no no. No you don't."

The man suddenly started shouting in her direction. Claudia was terrified that she had done something wrong.

"Get that mutt away from here." The man shouted, sounding furious.

"He's not a mutt." Someone from behind Claudia shouted back towards the man "I've told you before Percy, he's a highly trained dog."

Well that answered one question, the grumpy gardener was clearly called Percy. Now if this new man was called Neville then Claudia would be delighted.

"Get away from here Neville." Percy shouted back.

Bingo, this was exactly the man she was looking for. Neville strode confidently down into the gardens, apparently not even noticing Claudia was there. He looked very similar to Percy with same hair and beard but was wearing a red tunic decorated with white crosses. Walking by Neville's side was a red dog, a cocker spaniel if Claudia was not mistaken. The dog looked a very friendly and well behaved animal but hardly highly trained like Neville claimed.

"Get that thing away from my roses." Percy continued.

"Don't stand in the way of progress Percy, this is bigger than either of us." Neville replied.

"He's a lousy mutt Neville and you know it."

"This is not a mutt. Warwick here is the world's first and only metal detecting dog. If he's brought me here it means there is treasure to be found."

"There's no treasure here Neville. There wasn't any treasure last time you dug up my roses, there wasn't any the time before that and there won't be any treasure next time you bring that lousy mutt down here."

"You can't stand in the way of a treasure hunting dog Percy, it's just not how it works."

The two men were now stood right in front of each other. Claudia wondered if this very conversation had happened before, and if so, how many times.

"Stay away from my roses." Percy said angrily.

There were a few seconds of silence as the two men looked each either directly in the eyes. Eventually Neville broke the silence with an instruction to the dog.

"Treasure, Warwick. Dig for treasure."

Warwick the dog leapt forward and began sniffing around the roses. Percy was now shouting his objections towards Neville and Warwick but it had no impact at all. Warwick had obviously found something and began digging. Percy had been right to be worried about his roses as they soon became victims of the dogs digging. Warwick stuck his nose into the soil and came up holding something in his mouth. By the way it glistened in the sun it appeared to be metal.

"Good boy Warwick. Good treasure." Neville said with pride in his voice.

"My roses, you've destroyed my roses again." Percy seemed justifiably upset.

"Worth it for the treasure."

"That isn't treasure. That's a buckle off a shoe."
"Ah yes, but whose shoe buckle is it? Could it be Napoleon's or Alexander the Great's or maybe it's the shoe buckle of Mary Queen of Scots."

"How could it Alexander the Great's shoe buckle? How would Alexander the Great's shoe buckle end up in this garden in York you buffoon?"

The insult obviously upset Neville.

"I'm no buffoon you snivelling guttersnipe."

"You blithering twerp."
"Halfwit"

"Nincompoop."

The final insult stopped Neville in his tracks. The two stood nose to nose again looking square at each other. Eventually Neville narrowed his eyes and admitted defeat.

"OK. You win this round. Well played sir, well played."

Claudia had no idea how Percy had won this round, or even what game they were playing. Either way, Neville seemed to accept that his opponent had got the better of him.

"Come on Warwick. We have been beaten here. Drop the treasure boy. We don't deserve it."

Warwick dropped the shoe buckle and trotted after his master who was marching away from the gardens and muttering. Claudia followed after them.

"I know a great place to go and search for treasure." She said to Neville after she had caught up with them.

"OK, let's go there then." Neville replied "I'll show him, I'll prove him wrong. We'll be back here with all the treasure and show him what's what. Then he wouldn't be able to hit with that nincompoop manoeuvre."

Claudia led them down North Street and Skeldergate towards Cromwell Road and onto Baille Hill with Neville never once stopping his rant about Percy and his roses. Claudia wondered again how often they had gone through the same routine, the same arguments, and the same fights. She even wondered how often Warwick the great treasure hunting dog would find exactly the same shoe buckle.

At one time Baille Hill may have been an important part of the city like her mother said. However right now it was nothing but a small hill a few metres high and covered in trees.

"I bet that Percy has followed us." Neville continued "He's determined to stop me finding my treasure."

"Well I'm sure we'll see him if he has followed us." Claudia replied "Right, so if we head up to the top here we should be able to find something."

Claudia led the three of them up the hill but Neville was losing interest in her fast. He was too busy looking around for his enemy Percy who he was convinced had followed them down there.

Claudia had an idea. Lazily and with barely any attempt to hide what she was doing, she picked up a stone and threw it down the hill when Neville wasn't watching. The stone made a rustling noise as it rolled downwards through the grass and leaves.

"What was that?" Neville looked around desperately.

"I think I just saw a man down there." Claudia lied to Neville.

"Right, I've got him now. Come here you weasel, I've definitely got you now." Neville shot down the hill looking for Percy.

With Neville out of the way Claudia could begin searching for the key.

"Treasure, Warwick. Dig for treasure." She gave the dog instructions.

Warwick began searching around the hill, sniffing the ground looking for metal. Claudia wondered what he would unearth. Another shoe buckle maybe, or perhaps a button or a child's toy car. Well he'd certainly found something as he began digging for metal. Warwick stopped digging and stuck his nose into the soil. As before he came up with something in his mouth, something metallic that was glistening in the sun. Claudia went towards the dog and hoped for the best.

"Drop Warwick. Good boy" She said.

Claudia held out her hand and Warwick dropped his treasure into it. Sure enough it was the red key that she had been looking for. It was a fairly large key about the size of her hand and despite having been buried underground for many years, it looked perfectly clean and shiny as if it was brand new.

"Good boy Warwick. Good boy" She said giving the dog a hearty scratch behind the ear as a reward.

"He got away, the weasel. No sign of him at all." Neville had come back up the hill "Come on Warwick, we need to go."

Neville had seemed to have entirely forgotten about Claudia's promise of treasure. He hurried back down the hill and quickly made his way out of her sight with his faithful metal detecting dog at his side. Claudia looked down at the key in her hand. She'd done it.

*

"I've actually found it this time. I've found the red key." Claudia said to Balthazar whilst holding out the evidence triumphantly.

"Well done you." He replied with a hint of pride. "That's one key that the Queen of Shadows won't be getting her hands on."

"Yes indeed. One down, three to go."

"So you've found the key for Micklegate Bar, which is fantastic. So we still need the keys for Walmgate Bar, Bootham Bar and Monk Bar. Would you like me to keep hold of this key?"

"Yes please. I think that would be best."

"Fine stuff. Well you'd best get back to your own world. You can't stay here forever."

Claudia and Balthazar made their cheery goodbyes and Claudia began heading back towards where she had left her mother. She was so happy to have made progress and found the first key. Up until that point, Claudia had been wondering why Mathilda had suggested finding Balthazar to help her in her quest. However, now that she realised that Mathilda had been absolutely correct and Balthazar was the perfect man to be helping her out. He'd known exactly who would be able to help her find the key and exactly where he could be found.

Feeling fully contented Claudia headed back to find her Mother and get back to her own world. Oh yes her Mother! Claudia had completely forgotten all about her. So much had happened since she last saw her it really had been quite an adventure. Claudia returned to the point that she had last seen her and there her Mother was, standing in exactly the same place that she had left her. In fact, her Mother was still giving her lecture about York's castles.

"...and then in the 18th Century, all of the bailey buildings at which surrounded Clifford's Tower were knocked down and the whole area was turned into a prison. It remained a prison until the early 20th Century and now it is the museum. Oh sorry honey, I got a bit carried away there. I didn't mean to bore you, I know how much you hate local history."

"It's Ok Mum. It can be helpful sometimes."

Chapter 9 York Minster

"The Cathedral and Metropolitical Church of St. Peter in York, this is the proper name of the huge building better known as York Minster. Cathedral means the seat of a Bishop or in this case a highly ranked Archbishop. Metropolitical simply meaning that it is found in a city rather than in a more remote abbey. It was first built as a small wooden building in 627AD and soon became the minster church for the local area. In the very early days of churches in this country there was not a church in each village, instead all of the local priests were based in a minster church and went out preaching from there. In England there are 12 churches that date back to this time and are allowed to call themselves minsters, some are still small buildings but others have been built bigger and bigger and are now grand and imposing."

Charles Wellbeloved's Encyclopaedia of All Things York, Page 51

*

"Non Angli sed Angeli, Aella Halleluiah."

More roaming Friars chanting their way across the other York.

"Non Angli sed Angeli, Aella Halleluiah."

Which were these? It was a very similar sounding chant than the Blackfriars she had met with Mathilda but even without speaking Latin Claudia could tell that these were different words.

"Non Angli sed Angeli, Aella Halleluiah."

Round the corner came the Friars. As she suspected, these weren't the same as before. Whereas before all the monks had been wearing black habits, this time all of the men wearing grey habits. Claudia gave the Greyfriars a good look over. Each man had his hood up way over his head and was looking towards the ground as he walked. As such, it was impossible to see any of their faces. There was still so much about this Echo World that confused Claudia. She shook her head to try and clear the fog and headed out towards the library to speak to Lucy Cavendish.

"Hello Claudia, how are you today?"

"I'm doing well thank you Lucy, how are you?"

"I'm fine thank you? How did you get on with figuring out that map?"

Claudia still wasn't sure about speaking to Lucy about the map. Balthazar had been so clear about not trusting anybody. On the other hand, she couldn't think of anybody else who could help.

"The map? Oh yes, I'd forgotten about that." She tried her best to downplay her interest in it. "Well I never got my head around those cryptic clues. I've been thinking about what you were saying about anagrams and wondering if there was anything that might tell you if a clue has an anagram in it?"

"Oh, good question." Lucy replied in deep thought. "From what I remember there are some words that if you see in a cryptic clue then you know there is an anagram in there?"

"Right, what sort of words?"

"I'm not sure really, words about mixing up the letters to rearrange them. If the clue contains words such as 'mixed up' or maybe 'shaken' or 'crazy' or 'disorderly', that would tell you that you should shake up the letters to make other words."

Claudia looked through the three remaining clues for any words that might mean that there was an anagram.

"What about wild? Can 'wild' mean we need to rearrange some letters?" She asked

"Possibly. I'm not an expert but it certainly sounds about right."

"Right so what's the full clue? For a wild test, eat thirty."

"Hang on" Lucy had an idea "What I'll do is write each letter on a piece of paper so we can move them around and try to make other words."

The two of them spent some time looking for new words from the pieces of paper in front of them, starting with the letters in the words 'eat' and 'thirty'. Lots of words appeared to them that seemed promising, words like 'heart', 'they', 'treat' and 'earth'. At one point Claudia got very excited when she saw 'Yeti' but no matter how they arranged the letters they could not decipher the code. They decided to add in the letters for 'test' to see if that helped.

"What about 'artist'?" Claudia asked picking out the relevant pieces of paper and laying them out to form the word. "Were there any famous artists in York?"

"There was one." Lucy replied with a smile as she rearranged the remaining letters.

Claudia looked down at the words in front of her. They read 'Etty the Artist'.

"Etty the Artist?" she asked quizzically.

"William Etty was a successful artist who lived in York 200 years ago. I don't know what it's got to with anything but it's too much of a coincidence if it has nothing to do with him."

"Oh, I'm sure it means something to someone. I've no idea myself what it's about but I enjoyed the game. Thanks for your help Lucy, it's been a lot of fun."

Claudia waited until Lucy had left her and excitedly opened up her copy of Wellbeloved's Encyclopaedia for what it had to say about Etty the Artist.

"William Etty 1787 – 1849.

York born artist who was elected a fellow of The Royal Academy and achieved some success with his historical paintings. Further success may have come his way if his paintings had contained more people with their clothes fully on. Later in life he returned to York and set up a school of art. Etty also campaigned extensively to save the city walls and medieval bars that had been threatened with destruction."

Charles Wellbeloved's Encyclopaedia of All Things York, Page 270

The last sentence really piqued Claudia's interest. This man was clearly linked to the city walls and their preservation. It seemed very appropriate that he'd been entrusted with one of the Peterkeys. There was one small problem of course, it was slightly inconvenient that he died in 1849.

*

"Very good work as ever Young Claudia."

Balthazar once again seemed impressed when Claudia had told him what she had found. She had gone through her research and thought process in great detail but made sure to not mention Lucy at all. Claudia thought it best to pretend that she had done all the work alone, not out of arrogance but so that Balthazar wouldn't question how much information she had shared with someone else.

"I think you have definitely solved one of the other clues." He continued

"So how do I get the key?" She asked "If Etty died in 1849, where do I find him?"

"Good question." He thought about it for a second. "There is a statue of Etty outside the art gallery in Exhibition Square, you can go and speak to him there."

"Speak to a statue?" Claudia asked in surprise.

"Oh yes, have you never spoken to a statue before? Be careful though, being a statue is a lonely business. He probably hasn't spoken to anyone for a long time and so he might have gone a little odd over the years. If I were you I would try flattery. Make a really big deal of what he great job he did saving the walls and how important he is to the history of York. It might work, although I can't guarantee it."

*

Claudia wandered through the city on the way out to the art gallery. Lost deep in thought she realised that she could hear music. Sweet, heavenly music that was spilling out of The Minster and washing all over her. She walked up to the building and saw that the large wooden doors at the west end of the building were open wide The Minster's organ was playing on the inside. Loud, slow notes drifted out of the church into the streets of York, tempting and willing Claudia to go inside.

Claudia had been inside York Minster many times before. Her mother had dragged her in over and over, giving her lectures about the history and how it was one of the three largest medieval churches in Northern Europe and one of the top ten visited tourist attractions in England. That might all be true but right now it was…empty. There were no tourists wondering around with open mouths admiring the majesty of the surroundings, no staff rushing around making sure everyone was happy and behaving themselves, no priests trying to get on with their day job. Even the Archbishop of York who occasionally graced the building with his presence was nowhere to be seen. There was just her and the music.

With no one else in there the giant building looked absolutely immense. The walls and floors were decorated with delicately carved stone created hundreds of years earlier by immensely skilled medieval hands. Way above head were beautifully decorated wooden roofs and each wall was covered in massive stained glass windows.

Despite the huge space inside the building, the music seemed to be doing everything it could to fill it. She could both see and hear the notes of the music rising up high towards the roof. Crotchets bounced off stone columns and walls whilst minims bombarded the stained glass windows and explored the crevices and spaces of The Minster. Sunlight streamed through the windows on the south side of the church lighting up the notes in the midday sun. Claudia wandered up towards the organ in the centre of the cavernous space. She reached the middle of the building and looked up the inside of the central tower to watch the musical notes drifting up more than 70 metres above her up the inside of the tower towards the very top before fading out of view.

The music was definitely coming from the organ although there seemed to be no evidence of anyone who might be playing it. The huge pipes of the organ that were needed to make such a sound reached up towards the roof and below the pipes there was The Screen of Kings.

Every time she went into The Minster her mother dragged her over to the Screen of Kings. It was made up of 15 intricately detailed, life size statues of Kings of England starting with William the Conqueror and finishing with Henry VI. They had been carved from white stone nearly 600 years before Claudia first saw them and were finished with touches of gold paint. Each King had his name written at the base of the statue and each statue was unique although most had crowns, expensive robes and luxurious curled hair and beards. Many carried swords and others carried sceptres or crosses. Some looked stern, others distracted and one or two even looked angry.

The tune that the organ was playing was slow and rose and fell like the swelling of an ocean. The statues of the Kings were moving along to the music and it came as no surprise to Claudia when they began to sing.

Williams, Henrys and Edwards

Richards and Stephen and John

Though the world it keeps marching onwards

Our time at the top has long gone

We were the wealthiest in the nation

Had crowns and jewels and rings

Now we stand silently in formation

The Stone Carved Choir of Kings

Our armies obeyed our commands

We were lords of all we surveyed

And our swords still rest in our hands

Awaiting for those who need aid

Carved by finest stonemasons

Ready for all that life brings

We stand with infinite patience

The Stone Carved Choir of Kings

Were these statues offering themselves as defenders of the city if people needed help? More importantly, were they offering themselves specifically to Claudia? She wondered if she would need their help later. She sure hoped not.

As the voices of the Stone Carved Choir of Kings faded away, Claudia kept on walking past the central tower towards the East End of the building.

This part of The Minster was filled with tombs, monuments and dedications to important people who had been buried here. She walked to the left of the organ and realised that someone else was there, sat perfectly still in the shadows as if entirely unaware that anything was going around them. It was a lady wearing long, flowing robes that reached all the way to the floor and were lined with sumptuous purple velvet. Her dark robes were luxuriously decorated with gold stitching and on her head she wore a long white veil.

Claudia looked at her for a moment, trying to get a sense of who this lady was. Her clothing and demeanour were elegant and she gave off a sense of wealth and importance.

"Excuse me, may I sit down here?" Claudia asked as politely as she could.

"Of course you can dear." The lady replied.

She spoke in an accent that Claudia did not recognise. It sounded European but not like anything else she had heard before. Thinking back to Yves, Claudia wondered if she was even speaking English.

"I'm sorry to ask but where do you come from?" As she said it, Claudia felt embarrassed in case she sounded rude and so hastily added "It's just that you've got such a lovely accent."

"The country I come from no longer exists." The lady replied.

That answered that then. The lady seemed quite happy to speak but had not once turned or looked at Claudia. Worried that she getting nowhere with this line of questioning, Claudia tried something else.

"If you're not from this country then how come you are in this cathedral?"

"I was married here." The lady seemed more forthcoming on this topic, although she still didn't look at Claudia. "It was a long, long time ago but this was the site of my wedding. The place looked very different then, in fact they were still building it."

"Who did you marry?"

"Someone very powerful."

"Were you powerful yourself?"

"In my own way. In my time I could lead armies into battle, or I could spare people their lives if that is what I wanted."

Claudia wondered what sort of situations would lead to these decisions being made.

"Which was more important, fighting battles or sparing lives?" She asked

"I always told my children that it's not important what you do as long you feel it is the right thing for everyone and not just the easiest thing for you. And you should never, ever wait around for someone else to do it for you."

"You were a mother then, a long, long time ago?"

Finally the lady turned and looked directly at Claudia. She spoke calmly but firmly

"Young lady, once you become a parent you never stop being one. Yes I was a mother a long, long time ago and I am still a mother now. No matter what happens to my children, I will always be their mother."

"Even after they have fully grown?"

"They could be young, old, rich, poor, powerful or weak, they could even be a Duke or Countess but sooner or later everyone needs their parents. And their parents should always have time for their children, no matter what."

"I'm not sure my mother always has time for me." Claudia bemoaned "She always too busy giving lectures about Vikings."

The lady looked Claudia directly in the eye and thought for a couple of seconds. Claudia couldn't help but feel intimated by this powerful lady who had led armies into battle.

"I've met a lot of people your age." The lady eventually said "And they all feel hard done by their families. Their parents are either too controlling or not caring enough, their parents are either too distracted by other things or too interfering in their children's life. There is absolutely no way that any parent can do the right thing. But then young people grow up, have children of their own and realise that maybe their parents weren't so bad after all."

Claudia felt guilty. She was always so quick to criticise her mother these days. She often found herself thinking that her mother was too busy, not interested in enough in Claudia's life, too obsessed with this stupid city and its stupid history. Deep down she knew her mother cared for her and how lucky she was to have such a supportive and loving family.

"It's time for me to go." The lady said.

As the lady stood up, Claudia got the full blast of the majesty of the lady's clothing. The flowing robes, purple velvet and gold thread all gave an overwhelming sense of power and importance. If she did have the position of influence that she claimed she had then she must have been very intimidating to all of those around her.

"Will you be back?" Claudia asked

"I'm sure we will meet again."

Chapter 10 Exhibition Square

Lucy Cavendish was worried. She was worried about her young friend Claudia Ding. Lucy had known Claudia and her mother for a long time but only recently found out that Claudia could enter the Echo World. It had been exciting, if not at entirely surprising development and had made Lucy happy. However every time she saw Claudia she seemed obsessed with that map in her copy of Wellbeloved. Lucy was beginning to regret ever having suggested Claudia read the book in the first place, let alone encouraged her to solve those clues. It really wasn't ideal, not ideal at all. She would have to speak to somebody about this.

*

Claudia made her way out towards the city's art gallery where she planned to talk to a statue of artist William Etty in the hope that he would give her a key to the city gates. Saying it out loud like that made it sound a bit crazy.

She arrived outside the gallery and looked around her. She was stood in an area called Exhibition Square with the art gallery directly in front of her and Bootham Bar, one of the medieval gateways to the city, directly behind her. She had looked in her copy of Wellbeloved's Encyclopaedia and found out that the square had been created in the 19th century after a small stretch of the city walls had been demolished to allow a new road to be built. She also read that that the reason why a larger section of the walls hadn't been knocked down at the same time was because of a campaign to save them led by a local artist called William Etty. This was all useful information to her. Wellbeloved's book also had some copies of some of Etty's artwork that would be useful to look through.

Just next to the art gallery there was a very old brick and stone building, now part of the university and known as King's Manor. Claudia noticed that there were some gardens that she had never seen before. Usually there was nothing there but a tarmac road and a steady stream of students heading for lectures and gawping tourists being shown around by tour guides. Claudia wandered up to the door and saw the elaborate carving above it that her mother had repeatedly tried to talk to her about. The stonework was a square roughly two metres across and two metres high filled with 3 dimensional renderings of all sorts of highly detailed lions, unicorns, crowns, flowers, harps and writing. Not that she could read the writing, it appeared to be in a foreign language, but she could appreciate the bright colours that the whole thing had been painted in. Golds, reds, silvers, whites, blues and greens all adorned the craving and made a real impression. No time to spend on it today though.

She found a bench and began looking through the copies of William Etty's paintings. She was disappointed that all of the pictures in her book had rather boring names like *The Plantation at Acomb*, *Monk Bar* and *Preparing for a Fancy Dress Party*. The paintings were all fine but she couldn't help to think that the names of the paintings not shown in the book all sounded much more interesting. Names such *The World Before the Flood*, *The Wrestlers* and *Female Bathers Surprised by a Swan*. She wondered why these other weren't shown. The painting of Monk Bar looked like a good place to start, in fact it seemed perfect. A picture of one the entrances to the medieval city of York, one of the gateways that she was expecting to find a key for. The blue key in fact. The blue key that she thought she had just solved the clue for. "For a wild test eat thirty" was the clue which she rearranged to get "Etty the Artist". The man who had helped save the walls from destruction.

"What are you reading?"

She was so engrossed in the book she didn't even notice anyone near her. She looked up and saw a young women in a long and green dress that was studded with jewels as well as a string of pearls around her neck and a white headdress. Her clothes made her look like someone out of a picture book about the Tudor period and she certainly looked at home in the gardens of an old building like this.

"Oh sorry" Claudia said hurriedly "Just looking at some paintings."

"Really. Any paintings of me?" The women replied with a smile.

"I don't think so." Claudia said uncertainly "And if I did see paintings of you, what name would I be looking for?"

"Why I am the Queen of course. Queen Catherine. Surely you recognise me."

"Of course yes" Claudia lied "I was just...the sun was in my eye...I wasn't sure....sorry."

"That is fine. It's not often that you get to meet the Queen in person. And this is my first trip to York. My husband has been here before of course, and his family. In fact when his parents got married the city celebrated by putting in stained glass to the large circular window on the south side of The Minster that is known as a rose window."

"What were the pictures that they put in the stained glass?"

"Roses of course. Lots of pictures of roses to go in a rose window."

"Oh. Yes, well it makes sense now you say it."

"But they were special roses. You see my husband's father, King Henry VII was a member of a family whose symbol was a red rose. His family had long been fighting another family whose symbol was a white rose. But King Henry's wife, my husband's mother, was from the white rose family. Their wedding was celebrated as an end to the wars and the beginning of a new period of England. A new rose was created, a rose that was both red and white and celebrated a new united England."

"That's nice." Claudia said with a smile "Did you and your husband come here to York as well."

"Yes we did" Queen Catherine replied proudly "We came here in 1541. I remember it very well."

"And was your husband one of the people in the Screen of Kings in The Minster."

"Oh no. They'd been there for a hundred years or so before we even got there. No they're much older than us. We stayed here though, in this building. In fact that is why this building is called King's Manor."

"It wasn't always a house for the King?"

"Not at all. Originally it was a house for an Abbot, the important monk who was in charge of the monastery that was near here. An Abbot is of course not nearly as important as a King so when we stayed here they had to massively rebuild the place to make it bigger, grander and more important. More in keeping for a place for us Kings and Queens to stay in."

"Was the Abbot no longer living here then."

"No. My husband shut down all the monasteries and got rid of all of the monks and the abbots."

"Your husband shut down all of the monasteries?"

"Yes."

"All of the monasteries in England?"

"Yes all of them."

Claudia had a realisation. She had heard about the king who had shut down the monasteries in England. A king who was famous for having a big ginger beard and marrying lots of times.

"Was you husband King Henry VIII?" She asked

"Yes he was. The most powerful and important King around."

"Didn't he have lots of wives?"

"Well yes I'm not his first wife." Queen Catherine said with an air of embarrassment "I'm his fuff wiff"

She had trailed off so badly that Claudia had not been able to hear the end of her sentence properly.

"Sorry, I didn't catch that. Could you repeat what you just said?" Claudia asked hurriedly adding a respectful "Your Majesty."

"I'm his fifth wife." Queen Catherine repeated more clearly and with an air of defiance.

Claudia remembered that Henry VIII had 6 wives in total. She also knew a rhyme about his wives and what happened to them. Divorced, beheaded, died, divorced, beheaded, survived. Right, so Catherine was the 5th wife so that was divorced, beheaded, died, divorced, behead……oh no. This wasn't good, not good at all. She thought it would be best not to share this information with the queen. Especially as she didn't seem aware of what was going to happen.

"And are you happy with the King?" She choose to ask instead.

"Very happy. Very, very happy." Catherine was defiant again. "I mean, he's a lot older than me. He's 50 and I'm only 18. And he's not in very good health. And he's very overweight. So he just really lets me get on with my own thing, spend time with people of my own age. That sort of thing."

"And he doesn't mind you doing that. He doesn't get jealous at all?"

"No. Not that I know about anyway. As I say, he just lets me get on with my own thing. I don't really speak to him too much."

Claudia looked at Queen Catherine. She was young wasn't she? Very young. She was several years older than Claudia of course but still a girl in many ways. And Claudia could fully imagine a much older husband getting jealous of his young wife spending all her time with people of her own age. Whatever happened, it obviously didn't end well for Queen Catherine. Claudia suddenly felt that she needed to get away. Knowing what she knew about this young woman was making her feel uncomfortable.

"It was a pleasure to meet you, Your Majesty" She said with a curtsey "But I'm afraid I have to go now."

"Of course. It was pleasure to meet you as well"

"Oh and Your Majesty, please be careful."

Claudia left King's Manor and went back towards the art gallery leaving Queen Catherine looking puzzled at her parting words. But she couldn't dwell on this, she had an artist to speak to and a key to find.

Claudia had gone out to the gallery via the library and Lucy Cavendish had been kind enough to lend her a sketching pad and a set of pencils. She held them out ostentatiously in front of her, determined that if anybody should see her then they would mistake her for a serious artist. In front of the gallery there was a fountain containing a small pool of water, around 10 metres long, 2 metres wide and 1 metre deep. Along the edges of the pool there were jets of water shooting out into the air and back towards the centre of the pool. Next to the fountain was the life size statue of Etty the Artist. He looked grand and important in his 19th Century formal clothing and carrying a brush and easel.

Claudia sat on the edge of the fountain and brandished her art materials. She had seen people who thought themselves proper artists before and began to mimic their actions. She looked back over Bootham Bar towards the city and the West End of The Minster, the two square bell towers and a large stained glass window known as The Heart of Yorkshire dominating all around it. Having tilted her head in every position she could think of, she began to put pencil to paper. Claudia was not the greatest artist in the world but was talented enough that if anyone glanced over her shoulder they would know exactly what she was trying to draw.

She had been sketching for a few minutes before she felt someone was watching her. This was exactly what she wanted and glanced towards the large statue that stood next to the fountain. The statue quickly turned its head away and pretended that it hadn't been looking her way. Claudia didn't acknowledge what had happened but continued her drawing. After another couple of minutes exactly the same thing happened again. And then again, and again and again. Claudia felt that the time was right.

"We are lucky to these lovely old buildings in York." She said out loud to no one in particular "I just wish I could do them justice. I've seen some lovely old paintings of York. Much better than anything I could ever do." There was no response but Claudia was convinced that she could see the statue shuffling nervously.

"There was one painting of Monk Bar that was probably one of the best paintings I have ever seen."
Almost there now. She could feel the fish on the end of the line, just wanting to be reeled in.

"I'm just glad these walls are still there. It could have easily all been pulled down in the name of progress. I wonder who we have to thank for them still being here."

"Me. Me. You can thank me." The statue finally blurted out. "I saved it. I saved it all. If it wasn't for me then it would all be gone."

"Oh really." Claudia replied trying to sound impressed.

"Oh yes. When these roads were being built, the plan was to knock down all of the walls and all the bars to allow easy access to the city. I led the campaign to keep as much of the walls as possible."

"And people listened to you?"

"I'm a pretty important person around here." The statue sounded very proud "The name's Etty. You've probably heard of me."

"Yes Etty the Artist. You're the world famous painter." Claudia did not enjoy lying but felt it was acceptable in this context.

"Well you probably know then that those lovely old paintings of York you were looking at were painted by me. Yes I truly was one of the greatest artist of my day."

"Definitely one of the greatest."

"But I was so much more than just a painter, I cared about my home city and made sure I left my legacy."

"You founded a school of art didn't you?"

"I did, so that some of the next generation can try to reach and the levels of greatness of people like me. And of course I saved the city walls. Single handed saved them from the pointless destruction in the name of progress."

Claudia knew full well that this man was exaggerating his achievements. She wondered if he had actually been like in this real life or whether as Balthazar had suggested, the loneliness of being a statue had sent him a bit odd. Maybe standing quietly alone day in day out with no-one to speak to would do this to anyone.

"Well I'm very grateful." She lied "I'm sure you were well celebrated in your own life."

"I'm here aren't I? I have been immortalised for ever in statue form. I was also granted the honour of being buried inside York Minster."

"I'll have to try and find your tomb next time I go in."

"Actually you won't find me in there. There was a........misunderstanding involving my will and there wasn't enough money left over for burial in The Minster. So instead I was given pride of place in my own tomb by St Mary's Abbey. People tell me it's a very grand memorial."

Claudia wanted to move the conversation on. She felt that left to its own devices the statue could talk about itself all day.

"I've got a book here that shows some of you paintings" She said holding up her copy of Wellbeloved. "But some of the pictures are not shown. Do you know why?"

"Because people are scared about seeing the human body." The statue replied proudly.

"Oh.......OOHHHH"

A penny had dropped for Claudia. This paintings not shown must have had too many pictures of people without their clothes on. Time to move the conversation on again.

"So you have been given this grand statue, were you celebrated in any other way for your work saving the walls?"

The statue did not respond. In fact, it had appeared to have not even heard the question.

"Because you must have deserved it." Claudia continued "I think that I'd have viewed you as the most trustworthy, honest, passionate and reliable men. A man who had the highest levels of integrity."

The statute of Etty was almost visibly swelling with pride. Claudia felt sure she was about to land another fish. Just one last bit of effort.

"You're definitely the sort of man that I would entrust any special tasks needed doing."

"Welllllllll........"

So nearly there now. Claudia stared intently into the statues eye's, willing him to just go on.

"Well...Well there was one task. Several years ago I was entrusted with the safekeeping of something very special."

"Oh yes, what were you keeping safe?"

"A key."

"A key?" Claudia repeated as if hearing this information for the first time.

"Yes, I was told to look after a key. I was the only one they could trust you see. I was told to look after it as safely as possible until someone came to retrieve it."

"And do you still have this key?"

"Of course." The statue seemed offended by the question "If Etty the Artist is entrusted with a task then Etty the Artist fulfils that task like no one else before him."

"So who are you supposed to give the key to?" Claudia asked in total innocence.

"To the person who has honesty in their soul." Etty replied grandly.

"Do I have honesty in my soul?"

"You certainly do."

"Can I retrieve the key then?"

"I don't see why not."

The statue of Etty the Artist waved his hand and the jets in the fountain below him immediately switched off. Then something began rising up from the centre of the pool. Slowly it reached above the surface of the water and Claudia got a good look at the object. It was a small model of a white swan. Well that swan would certainly have disturbed her if it appeared when she was bathing. Clearly sitting on top of the swan was a blue key, about the same size as the red key she had found earlier, glinting in the sun and looking fantastic. Claudia had done it, she had got the second Peterkey.

Chapter 11 King's Fishpond

"In the 15th Century there were two families fighting it out to be King of England. The Dukes of Lancaster whose symbol was a red rose and the Dukes of York whose symbol was a white rose. Nowadays we call these battles The Wars of the Roses and the white rose has been adopted as a symbol of York and Yorkshire. However at the time things were very different and the Dukes of York had very little land, influence or significance over the city with who they shared their name. In fact, the biggest landowners around the area were the Percy Family who were major supporters of the red rose Lancastrian Kings. The Percy Family had a long running rivalry with the Neville Family who were big supporters of the white rose Yorkist Kings. The two families provided so many troops and generals to the rival sides in these battles that some people have suggested that the Wars of the Roses should be renamed the Percy-Neville Feud. One man, Richard Neville the Earl of Warwick, was so wealthy and powerful that his own private army could decide who was going to be king. As such he is now known in history as Warwick the Kingmaker. Looking back now, their arguments may seem confusing, pointless and a bit ridiculous but to the people involved at the time they were all deadly serious."

Charles Wellbeloved's Encyclopaedia of All Things York, Page 156

*

"The blue key"

Claudia could not help but sound proud as she held out her latest discovery for Balthazar to look over.

"Very impressive." He replied "How did you get him to hand it over?"

"Now that would be giving away my secrets wouldn't it." She said with a smile.

"So that's two down and two to go. Would you like to me to look after this one as well?"

"I think that would be best yes."

"And have you got any further with solving the clues for the other two keys?"

"Not yet but I have been thinking about the Queen of Shadows."

"Oh yes?"

"Well I met a very mysterious lady earlier who was sat in the shadows inside The Minster. To be honest, I found her really intimidating. She was wearing this rich purple velvet gown and well...."

Her voice trailed off as she felt the withering glare of Balthazar upon her.

"Purple velvet." He repeated slowly.

"So the way she was sat in shadows inside The Minster and her dark clothes and ...well...well...she might be....shadows."

By the time she stopped speaking, Claudia's words were barely audible. She felt stupid. Of course this lady wasn't the Queen of Shadows, how could she ever have thought that it was? Claudia tried another track.

"What if Mathilda faked her own kidnapping. She always wears black, so calling herself the Queen of Shadows could be...maybe she's trying...maybe."

Even as she was speaking she knew that Balthazar was not going to be impressed.

"Listen Claudia." He said slowly and deliberately "When you meet the Queen of Shadows then I'm sure that you will know exactly who she is and why she deserves her name. It won't be Mathilda, it won't be your friend Lucy Cavendish and it won't be me in a dress. There won't be any twists or turns. This is a very serious situation and we should be focussing on what we can do to help, which is finding the Peterkeys. You've done amazingly well to find these two so let's not get distracted and just concentrate on solving the last two clues."

Claudia felt put in her place, about three inches tall and a little bit thick. She couldn't wait to get out of there and back to her home world.

*

"Hi Lucy how are you doing?" Claudia said brightly as she walked into the local history section of the library the following Saturday.

"Hello Claudia, I'm fine thank you. I hope you're well." Lucy Cavendish replied

"Oh I'm doing very well. Very well indeed."

"How are you getting on with decoding that map?"

"Well that's what I would like to ask about."

"Oh, well fire away. What do you want to know?"

"This part of the city on the east side of York." Claudia said pointing to the map of York she found in Wellbeloved's Encyclopaedia. "A couple of things. Firstly there are no walls there on the map, I know there aren't any walls in that area by Foss Islands in my world but if this map shows the walls as they originally were, shouldn't the original walls there?"

"OK, well I can answer that easily enough. But before I do, what's the second thing?"

"The map has an area that is marked as 'The Kings Fishpond (Sometimes)'. So what does that mean?"

"Good questions." Lucy said with a smile "Well there were never any walls on that stretch on the East side of York."

"But I thought that the walls went all the way around the city. Wouldn't that leave one side of the city open to attack?"

"Well if there were no other defences than absolutely yes."

"So there must have been other defences on that side of York."

"Good deduction. Let me take you back to when the castle was first built."

Oh no. Another lecture about the castle.

"When the castle was first built the rivers were dammed to create a moat so that around the base of Clifford's Tower there was deep water. The trouble was, doing that also accidentally created a lake further up the river."

"A lake called 'The King's Fishpond' by any chance."

"Absolutely correct. So if there is a large lake and muddy ground on the east side of the city you don't need walls. Nobody is going to able to get across without being very vulnerable to attack by the soldiers defending the city."

"Aah right. That makes a lot of sense. So why does the map say Sometimes?"

"Well the fishpond has long since dried up in your world. If someone was to go down there there'd find pretty much no trace of a lake at all. But in the echo world it is still there…sometimes"

"Sometimes?"

"Well you know how this world works. Sometimes it's there and sometimes it isn't. It's usually there when you want to find it but not there if you don't."

"Right. And where would I go to find the fishpond?"

"Just head down The Stonebow and onto Peaseholme Green. The pond should be there. Or not. It depends.

"Depends on what?"

"Whether it's there or not."

"OK. I guess that's clear. Is it worth going to find it?"

"Not really."

"But it wouldn't be dangerous to go there?"

"Not as far as I know." Lucy thought for a second "There are the pirates but I think they're safe enough."

"Pirates!" Claudia's eyes opened as wide as they could.

"Well they call themselves pirates." Lucy continued "As I say they're pretty harmless."

This day had suddenly got a whole lot more exciting. Claudia was going to go and meet some pirates. Pirates that might have treasure chests. The perfect place to keep anything really important ultra-secure. Really important things like precious keys.

Claudia headed down The Stonebow and Peaseholme Green just as Lucy had told her to do. Sure enough there was a lake there. There was even a wooden dock on the edge of the lake that she went to stand on. This had definitely not been there the last time she walked down there, or any other time she'd been into this part of the city. But it was here now and that was all that mattered.

She saw a small wooden rowing boat making its way towards her across the lake. There were two figures in the boat, one a large man in an elegant frock coat and a wearing a substantial white wig not dissimilar to one that a judge might wear. The other was a smaller man in rougher clothes, white bell bottom trousers and a blue shirt that made him look like a sailor from a picture book. The smaller man also had a scowl on his face and a general air of displeasure. Claudia could see why he might be upset as it was clear that the larger man was forcing the surly sailor to do all the rowing.

"Ahoy there" The larger man called out towards Claudia as they came in to the dock. "Can we give you a ride?"

"Yes, that would be nice" She replied.

"Lancelot Blackburne's the name," The larger man said as he helped Claudia aboard the boat "It's a pleasure to meet you young lady."

"Yes, a pleasure to meet you as well. My name is Claudia Ding."

"Well Claudia, settle yourself down and we'll get ourselves off. Come along Joseph" Blackburne addressed the Surly Sailor "Let's get going, can't wait here all day."

"I suppose I'm still doing the rowing am I?" Joseph the Surly Sailor complained

"I don't see any other sailors here. Now stop your griping and get on with it."

The Surly Sailor pushed them off and began rowing across the pond, grumbling and moaning the whole time.

"So what brings you to The King's Fishpond?" Blackburne asked.

"I was told that there might be pirates here." Claudia replied.

"Well you come to the right place then" The Surly Sailor said with a grin "Ain't she Cap'n Blackburne" "Quiet Joseph you scurvy dog, I don't pay you to speak."

"You dun't pay me at all Cap'n"

"Enough of your cheek. Get back to your rowing."

"If you're Captain Blackburne" Claudia asked with wide eyes "Does that mean that you're the pirates."

"Well I've certainly done some things in my life, things that I'm not proud of and need to atone for. And yes, like a lot of people in my younger days I may have done a little pirating. But then, who hasn't?"

" A little pirating? That sounds very vague. So it's that why you're here on The King's Fishpond, recapturing your younger days as a pirate? "

"Something like that. Either way it certainly beats the day job."

"And do you manage to get much pirating done out here?"

"Have a look around and see what you think."

"I can't see how you would" Claudia said giving the lake a good look over "There doesn't seem to be anyone else out here."

"That is a bit of a problem yes. You do get a few other boats out here, fishermen and the like, but there's hardly lots of opportunity about for pirating."

"So you wouldn't be the right people to speak to if say I was searching for some treasure."

"Ha." The Surly Sailor spluttered "Chance o' treasure would be fine thing."

"Quiet Joseph before I feed you to the fishes." Captain Blackburne shouted "No Claudia, we are not the people to speak to about treasure. Unless you're talking about the treasure of getting out on the water and spending time with your friends. Was that the treasure you were talking about?"

"No. Not really." Claudia had one shot left "I don't suppose you know anything about any keys?"

"No, I know nothing about any keys. Unless of course you're talking about singing a jaunty sea shanty in the key of E. Was that the sort of key you were talking about?"

"No. Not really."

Well that was all bit of a shame. She had come out here with such high hopes and left with nothing. They weren't even proper pirates, just an older man trying to recapture his youth. They had managed to row all the way across the Fishpond, well Joseph the Surly Sailor had rowed them across the pond, much to his annoyance as he still chuntered away. There was another wooden dock that they headed towards and pulled up alongside.

"Sorry to disappoint you young Claudia." Captain Blackburne said as he helped her out of the boat "However I'm sure that at some point in the future we may be of more use to you."

"Of course, thank you for your time. And I hope that you continue to enjoy coming here and recapturing your youth."
"I certainly will. As I said, it certainly beats the day job."

"What was your day job?"

"Oh, didn't I say? I was Archbishop of York."

Chapter 12 Minster Close

The hardest thing of all is admitting when you are wrong.

*

"Fratres, non sumus. Nos mendacium dicere."

Now which of the Friars was this? It didn't sound like the Greyfriars or the Blackfriars. Claudia strained her neck to get a good look.

"Fratres, non sumus. Nos mendacium dicere"

She saw a group of people passing the end of Stonegate all in brilliant white robes.

"I guess they must be the Whitefriars." She said out loud

"If you say so." Replied her companion.

Claudia was very hopeful that nobody in her own world could see her right now. Sat, as she was, in the middle of what is usually a busy shopping street and wearing a single glove like some sort of deranged popstar. The one friend she could totally rely on was currently laying on her lap as she stroked him and tickled him under the chin. The glove was for a very practical purpose, she needed to stop her hand getting scratched.

"You always seem so happy Stonecat." She said to her companion as he purred loudly

"And why wouldn't I be?" Stonecat replied.

"No reason at all I suppose. It's easy for you but I've still got loads on my mind. My friend is still missing, she's probably been captured and maybe imprisoned whilst I've still got two clues to solve and two keys to find."

"I'm a little confused about that." Stonecat said in puzzlement

"What are you confused about?"

"Why are you worried about your friend? As long as you are alright, why care about other people?"

Claudia shook her head and laughed. She couldn't entirely tell if Stonecat was being serious or not.

"You're a silly old cat aren't you?" She said to him

"Less of the old if you don't mind" He replied as he rolled onto his back and stretched out his legs.

"Your belly looks so tempting to tickle right now." Claudia said "Would you bite or scratch me if I tickled you?"

"I don't know." The cat replied "Let's find out."

Claudia thought about it for a while.

"I don't think I will." She eventually said

"Very sensible. I wouldn't if I were you. Why don't you just relax and forget about everything."

"I don't think I can. There is just too much going on in my head right now. Where's Mathilda? What is a sharp key? How can I search in the last will? There's also something that Balthazar said that is a really bothering me but I can't think what it was or why it's bothering me. Stonecat what I am I going to do? Don't pretend to be asleep, I know you can hear me. Would you help me Stonecat, if I needed you to defeat the Queen of Shadows?" The cat opened one eye

"What would be in it for me?" He asked.

"Well if The Queen of Shadows got hold of the keys then she could control the whole city. Maybe we would all be in danger from her."

"Oh I see. Well maybe I'd help, maybe not. I'm really far too sleepy to decide right now."

*

The fog had come down even faster this time. One second Claudia had been happily walking along Minster Close along the South side of The Minster, she and her mother both enjoying the unexpected autumn sunshine, the next second she was completely surrounded by mist.

But it was the silence that hit her more than anything else. There had been so much noise, chatter and sound all around her before the fog came. Young people of all nationalities were bustling around trying to take the perfect photograph of themselves with The Minster in the background, a busker was attempting to sing what her mother had described as a rather ambitious acoustic cover of David Bowie's song Heroes, there was even a wedding going on with guests spilling out of the smaller St Michael le Belfry church that is right next door to the large Minster building. And then the next second there was complete and utter silence. It hit her so hard that she nearly fell backwards. It was only when she started to hear the low drone of what she now realised were distant planes that she recovered her balance.

"Yves" she called out "Yves, are you there? I'm scared."

"Don't be afraid of the fog Claudia."

The figure of Yves emerged from the fog. Claudia felt reassured to see him with his impassive face, short neat hair and WWII pilot's uniform.

"Don't be afraid of the fog" He repeated.

"But I can't see where I'm going."

"That's not a problem. We can't always know everything. Sometimes you don't know where you are going."

"But how do I know I am going in the right direction?"

"You don't. You just have to do what you think is best. The fog will clear and when it does you might realise you are going wrong but you can always change course when you can see more clearly."

"But I like to know what I'm doing."

"We all like to know what we're doing but uncertainty is nothing to fear. Never trust anybody who claims to know everything. If someone can't admit that sometimes they can't see where they are going then they aren't being honest with themselves."

He smiled again, turned and faded into to the mist.

"Yves" Claudia called out again "Yves"

And then the fog was gone, the noise was back, a tourist nearly knocked Claudia over trying to get a photo, wedding guests laughed and cheered and the busker was claiming once again that we could heroes, just for one day.

"Are you alright honey? Did you just say something?"

Claudia's mother sounded concerned. Claudia quickly tried to clear her head and pretend that everything was alright.

"Yes Mum I'm fine. Just looking at that wedding over there."

"Oh yes funny isn't it. People are rarely allowed to get married in The Minster itself so they get married in St Michael le Belfry next door and then get their photos outside the doors of The Minster in a pretence that they had got married there instead. Well they got a nice day for it if nothing else."

Claudia had a thought. Maybe her mother's knowledge of York could come in useful after all.

"Has anyone ever got married in The Minster?"
"Yes. It's rare to get permission but it does happen."
"Has anyone important ever got married there?"
"King Edward the Third got married there. He married Philippa of Hainault."

"Hay-no?" Claudia repeated trying to match her mother's pronunciation.

"Yes Hainault. The country no longer exists and is mostly in Belgium now."

"A country that no longer exists. When did this happen?"
"In the 14th Century. Sometime in the 1320's. Maybe 1328 if I remember correctly."
Claudia didn't care about the exact date, all she cared about was that this took place a long time ago.

"What was Philippa like?" Claudia asked

Hopefully the description that came back would match the mysterious and slightly intimidating lady that she had met in the shadows inside The Minster.

"Philippa was a very interesting person. She was quite a dominant personality and very powerful in her time. The most famous story of her is when she persuaded her husband to spare the lives of a group of people called the Burghers of Calais. But she did so many interesting things."

"Did she ever lead troops into battle?"

"Erm…let's think. Yes I think she did actually. At the Battle of Neville's Cross in the 1340's. Yes, she was a very interesting lady indeed. When I was about your age I…erm…did a research project on her and learned a lot about her. She's one of the main reasons that I got interested in local history."

"When she got married, was that when they were still building The Minster."

"That's good memory. Yes, there has been a church here since 627 AD but the current Minster building was built between 1220 and 1472."

Claudia did some quick maths in her head.

"252 years to build it. Wow, that took a long time didn't it."

"Well it's a very big and intricate building and everything had to be done by hand so it took a really long time, and of course it is still constantly being repaired and restored. And these guys in the Stonemasons Hut over there are the people who do some of the restoration work."

They had walked all the way past the south side of The Minster, past the circular Rose Window that Queen Catherine had told her about and had reached the Stonemasons yard at the east end of the building. There were two men and a woman in the Stonemasons Hut, all working away on blocks of stone. Each one was very carefully chipping away at their block of stone by hitting a long metal chisel with a large hammer with a round stone head. Claudia looked at the finished blocks on the floor next to them and marvelled at the intricate detail that they had managed to create with such primitive tools.

"The stonemasons are the people who carved all of the stone into its correct shape." Her Mother went on. "The Master Mason was the most important person on a medieval building site because he was the one that directed all of the other workers in their tasks."

Claudia had stopped listening to her mother however, her attention had being entirely devoted to something else. She had realised that one of the stones that the masons had carved was of face and upper body of a man. He looked spectacularly and strikingly ugly and twisted. And there was no two ways about it, it was a statue of a man who was undoubtedly picking his nose.

"What's that?" She pointed at the man picking his nose

"It's called a grotesque" Her mother replied "It's similar to a gargoyle but a gargoyle really has to have a water spout in its mouth that stops the building being damaged by rain water. If it doesn't then it is called a grotesque but the idea is that if you have ugly or scary carvings on the outside of a church then the local people will be reminded of all of the evil in the world and that going inside is the church is the only safe way to protect from evil."

Claudia, could barely take her eyes of the grotesque. She wondered how she would have reacted if she had been a medieval peasant and had seen that on the side of a church. She definitely would have been scared by it but wasn't sure if it have driven her inside the church for protection.

"What's all the sudden interest in history and architecture then honey?" Her mother asked with a smirk on her face.

"No reason at all. I'm just interested."

"Just interested eh? Fair enough. So you'd be interested in St. William as well?"

"St. William?" Claudia repeated in confusion.

They had moved on from the Stonemason's Yard and gone past the east end of The Minster stopping outside another building. It was an old looking building with stone walls at ground level and an upper story sticking out slightly over the pavement. The upper story was made of white plaster and black wooden beams with a series of bay windows jutting out. As with other old buildings, the beams of wood all bowed and sagged and no 2 seemed to be the same length or width. Claudia and her Mother were standing outside of a pair of heavy wooden doors that had a carving of a man above them. The man was wearing a pointed hat, holding a crook and lifting his right hand up as if giving a blessing.

"Was he a bishop?" Claudia asked

"He certainly was. Good deduction. He was Archbishop of York in the 12th Century but was considered so holy and so important that he is now known as St. William of York. In the middle ages his body was in a tomb in The Minster and pilgrims used to visit his shrine and pray for miracles."

Claudia gave another look around, she noticed several things on the side building. There was a sign stating that the building was called St. William's College and there were two shields either side of the carving of William. The shield on the left was coloured gold and had a number of coloured diamonds on it, the other shield showed a pair of silver keys crossed over each other.

"What are the shields about?" She asked

"The gold one is William's own Coat of Arms, his own symbol that he used to display so that people knew it was him. The other shows the crossed keys of St. Peter. The Minster church is dedicated to St. Peter who of course holds the keys to the gates of heaven and so the crossed keys are the symbol of Peter and of The Minster."

Keys and Peter. That was interesting. Very interesting. Very interesting indeed. The name Peterkeys had been confusing her since she first heard it but now it was beginning to make sense. Plus she now had a good idea of where she could find one of the other missing keys. Especially after looking very carefully at the words 'St. William' on the side of the building.

"Why are you smiling honey?" Her mother asked.

"Oh, I think the fog is lifting" Claudia replied.

"Fog? Are you mad, it's been wonderfully sunny all day?"

Claudia's smile turned into a small laugh.

"Well we need to get on" Her mother continued "You want to go to this souvenir shop don't you and then where do you want to go?"

"Somewhere that sells art supplies."

"That's right. I still don't understand what you get up to, oh daughter of mine, but I'm glad you're finally taking an interest in your city."

Chapter 13 North Street

Meg Montgomery was worried. She was worried about her young friend Claudia Ding. Ever since Mathilda had introduced them Meg had enjoyed speaking to Claudia, her youthful enthusiasm and excitement with finding out about the echo world had made Meg feel young again. However, since Mathilda had gone missing young Claudia had become increasingly withdrawn and every time she came to the café she sat obsessively reading a copy of Wellbeloved's encyclopaedia. She seemed particularly interested in an old map. Not that she told Meg this of course, it was only what Meg had learned from looking over her shoulder. It really wasn't ideal, not ideal at all. She would have to speak to somebody about this.

*

"Claudia, come this way. I've got some people I'd like you to meet."

It wasn't exactly the welcome that Claudia was expecting as she stepped off the 415 bus for her usual Saturday trip around York. There was Lucy Cavendish, beaming brightly and beckoning her across the street. Claudia looked over to see whether her mother had also seen Lucy but whether she had or hadn't, she was rapidly fading out of view as Claudia went into the Echo World.

"Hello Lucy, I didn't expect to see you here." Claudia replied.

"No, I dare say you didn't. But if you follow me, I think you'll find these people interesting.

Claudia shrugged her shoulders and crossed the street, following Lucy down some steps towards a building that she had walked past every

Saturday for years. It was another old, medieval building with the familiar timber and plaster walls and the upper story jetting out noticeably above the ground floor. Like the old buildings she had seen in The Shambles or St William's College, Claudia reckoned that if you went around this building with a ruler you would not be able to find a single straight line. Wooden beams wibbled and wobbled their way up the sides of the building and the horizontal beams all looked bowed and bent out of shape. This place was bigger than the other buildings though and had smaller stone building stuck almost haphazardly onto one end as if someone had tried to repair the place with superglue. The plaster was different to other buildings as well, usually plaster was white but this plaster was a bright colour, a pinky orangey colour that stood out quite alarmingly.

Down at the bottom of the steps stood two ladies, one dressed in clothes that Claudia reckoned would make her from the mid-20th century and the other in clothes that her put her in the first part of the century. The lady from the early 20th century was wearing a huge hat in a style that Claudia had only ever seen on those who were campaigning for votes for women and that was so wide that Claudia could barely believe what she was looking at.

"This lady here is Maud Sellers" Lucy said gesturing towards the lady under the huge hat "And she can tell you all about this magnificent building.

"Hello Claudia" Maud said cheerily "Lucy has told us about you and about how interested you are about learning about this city. Well when I was a young a women, I too was fascinated by learning about the past and was determined that when I grew up I was going to be a historian.

Unfortunately, at that time women rarely got the opportunity to get the same sort of education as our brothers and husbands so I had to work extra hard and be extra good at what I was doing so that people had no choice but to take me seriously. That's how I got involved with this building. Do you know what it is?"

"Not really no. My mother has spoken about it before but I...well I wasn't really listening."

"That's fine. Well this building is, in a way, a symbol of how York became so rich and powerful. You see the hills surround the city of York are so full of wonderful resources such as stone, metals and most importantly of all sheep."

"Sheep?" Claudia asked in surprise.

"Of course sheep. Sheep are the absolute key to all of our riches. The farmers up in the hills kept the sheep healthy and then when the time is right sheared off the sheep's fleece, loaded them onto small wooden boats and sent the fleece off down the rivers into York. Here the fleeces were turned into fancy, expensive woollen cloth which was loaded up onto big sea faring ships and sent off to the rest of the world to sell and make a huge profit. A group of merchants who traded in the cloth and other luxury items, all banded together and called themselves The Merchant Adventurers. They're the ones who built this hall as a place where they could meet."

"The Merchant Adventurers? What a grand name that is." Claudia was impressed.

"Yes, well it was a name they gave themselves. They felt that because they were trading with people from far, far away they were really adventurous. Nowadays there is very little woollen cloth that is still made or traded in York but the Merchant Adventurers remain a powerful group of people acting to raise money for charity and other good causes. In 1913 I was elected to the society, the first women to be elected in their 500 year history, and set about writing the history of the group, collecting their archives and restoring this building. The building had fallen into a bad state of repair but over the years and I organised restoration and repair works on it to bring it back to its full glory. It's not easy restoring an old building you know. It takes a huge amount of time and effort."

"And that brings us to our second person here." Lucy interrupted and gestured towards the other lady. "This is June Hargreaves."

"Hello Claudia." June was just as friendly as Maud "Yes, I was working for York City Council in 1964 and realised just how easy it was at the time for people to knock down and destroy historic buildings in the name of progress. Obviously that would not do so I worked hard to make changes that would help us protect our history and the British Government later adopted my recommendations and changed the laws to bring in lots of new protections for historic buildings."

"If it wasn't for people like June and their campaigning then our historic towns and would be much different than they are today." Lucy said with obvious admiration in her voice.

"Afterwards I spent my life working to restore and protect many, many buildings here in York" June continued "But just as importantly, I realised that there was no point having all of these lovely old buildings if they are lying empty. You can't just live in the past, even a city like York with all of its echoes and reminders of the past needs to be a living, flourishing modern city with shops and restaurants and jobs and work. Finding the balance between the past, the present and the future is the most important thing for any city."

Claudia enjoyed talking with Lucy, Maud and June and the four of them chatted away for some time about the history and future of the city that they all loved. After a while, feeling full of confidence and optimism, Claudia decided to try and find Balthazar and discuss an idea she had had. It was only a short walk up Fossgate from The Merchant Adventurers Hall to the corner with The Stonebow and sure enough, the man in the white robes was easily found there. She went through her idea with him and waited for a response. She hoped it was going to be positive...

"So your plan is to go to the carving of St. William and ask him for the silver Peterkey?"

Claudia felt the full weight of Balthazar's gaze. He wasn't actually saying that she was stupid but every other part of his body and demeanour was telling her that this is exactly what he was thinking.

"Not just ask him" she said weakly "Ask him politely."

What was she thinking? Saying it out loud made the whole thing sound absolutely ridiculous. She looked at Balthazar. As always he was the epitome of a wise and authoritative older man. He looked down at her with his long, expressionless face and Claudia once again marvelled at his equally long white robes that were always so clean and bright that they had seemed to come out of an advertisement for laundry capsules.

"Talk me through the reasons again?" he asked slowly "Why do you think he has the key?"

 "The clue says 'Search inside the last will. I am sure you will find what you're looking for if you ask politely'. If you look at 'last will I am sure' then you'll see the words St. William."

"Yes...Ok."

""So if I ask him politely....he might have the key."

There was a few seconds silence before Balthazar spoke. When he finally did, he was calm, polite and respectful. Which only made things worse.

"Claudia. You have done fantastically well so far. Solving those first two clues was very intelligent and the way you worked with Neville and Etty to get the keys off them was very impressive. However, I do think that you're overthinking this clue. A last will and testament is a document that you write to detail what will happen to your possessions after you die. If you look through various last wills in the city archives I am sure that you will find someone detailing where the silver key is."

Claudia left Balthazar feeling low. She felt that she had to find some more friendly faces and headed up The Shambles. She saw Gus and Meg's shop laid out as a butchers, displaying all the sausages and chops that she thought would be attractive to meat eaters. However, by some process in this new world that she did not understand, by the time she reached the shop it had become a café advertising tea and cakes.

"Claudia." Gus called out "How good to see you."

"Is that Claudia." Meg called out from the back of the shop. "We haven't seen nearly enough of you recently. Any news of Mathilda."

"I'm afraid not no." Claudia replied.

She really felt like she would like to tell them about all that adventures she had been on around the keys and looking for Mathilda but as she opened her mouth she realised that nothing was going to come out.

"How's business?" she found herself saying instead.

Claudia, Gus and Meg proceeded to discuss the shop and some of the customers who had come by recently. They spoke cheerily and extensively and although Claudia wasn't really listening to what they were saying, she was very happy to speak to them. It was just nice to have a conversation with pleasant people about nothing in particular. The fact that she was offered a delicious piece of chocolate cake only made things better. As usual, Meg was trying to get Gus to believe ridiculous facts about York, such as the fact that their grandfather owned the city's first metal spoon or that the name of the city of York comes from what the locals call the yellow part of an egg. It was exactly what Claudia needed to take her mind off things.

The conversation only ended when another group of customers came their way. Not wanting to be in the shop as it returned to a butchers shop, Claudia made her excuses and left them to it.

"Lovely to see you Claudia, come back soon." Meg called after her as she moved away from the shop.

"Oh so this is the Claudia we've heard so much about" Came a different voice.

Claudia looked around. At first she thought that it was one of the customers at the shop who had spoken but they were all in deep conversation with Gus. There really wasn't anyone else around who could have said her name. Then she heard yet another voice.

"She doesn't look like she needs our help."

Once again she looked around but there was definitely no one at street level. It was only then that she thought about looking above street level. She looked up and there sat on window ledges above her were the two cats that she had once seen chasing each down The Shambles, one black cat and the other cat made out of white wool. As she looked up at them neither of them looked like they were going to say anything else but the way they were watching her convinced her that they were the sources of the voices that she had heard.

Someone was talking about her and trying to persuade others that she needed help. That was interesting.

*

Why wouldn't Balthazar listen to her? It was so obvious to Claudia that she should be speaking to St. William so why was he refusing to even consider that she might be right. She was also still convinced that the Queen of Shadows was the mysterious lady she had spoken to inside The Minster. The fact that she now thought that she knew the lady's name only made her more convinced that she had the right person. Nobody listening to you when you know that you've got the answer is the most frustrating thing in the world.

Balthazar had just said that she was overthinking things. That was so patronising. She'd already solved two of the clues and found two keys, so to be dismissed so quickly this time was quite frankly insulting. Having said that....maybe he had a point. Maybe, if she thought deep down, maybe she was overthinking things. Maybe she had to go back to what had made her successful before.

She'd found the first key with the help of a metal detecting dog named Warwick. Maybe if she could find the dog again, he could search out the other two keys. The last place she had found Warwick was in North Street Gardens. If she went back there he could be there again. Probably not but it was worth a go if nothing else.

Claudia walked through the city streets and over Lendal Bridge towards North Street Gardens. She was hoping to find Warwick the dog and his owner Neville in the gardens. She wondered if she would find Neville and his rival Percy in the gardens having another War of The Roses. She hoped so. That was fun last time.

In the end she was pretty disappointed to see neither of them in there. There was only one person in the gardens and although she did not recognise him, even with Claudia's limited historical knowledge she could tell straight away that he was a Victorian gentleman. The top hat, waistcoat, black bow tie and heavy coat were all dead give-away. He was not a particularly old looking man, maybe in his 40's but he had a real air of authority and seriousness about him. He had seen her looking at him.

"Good morning young lady." He said to her as polite as it was possible to be.

"Good morning sir" Claudia replied trying to match his politeness.

"And what is your name?"

"My name is Claudia Ding."

"Well it is a pleasure to meet you Claudia Ding, my name is Dr Snow."

Claudia was not surprised to hear this man was a doctor, it absolutely matched up with his clothing and manner.

"So what brings you to these gardens Claudia?" Dr Snow asked

"I was looking for some people I met here before. Do you know a man called Neville? He has a dog by the named Warwick."

"Yes I know Neville and Warwick, they come here fairly regularly to have their argument with Percy. Have you met Percy and Neville?"

"Yes I have."

"Ridiculous men aren't they."

Claudia laughed, the previously stern looking Dr Snow also smiled.

"Are you a medical doctor?" Claudia asked

"I certainly was." He replied

"Were you successful?"

"You could say that yes. There was once an outbreak of a disease, a disease that people no longer die of in this country but used to kill many, many people. No-one really knew what caused this disease at the time.

Many people said that the disease was carried in the air but I thought that the disease was carried in the water. I tried to convince others that it was the water that was the problem but people didn't believe me, they told me that I know nothing."

"So what did you do?"

"I found out the details of everyone who had got the disease, put all of them on a map and realised that everyone who was ill was getting their water from the same water pump. Just like this pump here."

As he spoke he reached out and touched the hand operated water pump that Percy was using last time she was here.

"Did they believe you then?" Claudia asked with wide eyes and an air of excitement.

"Well some people did but not everybody. So we went out and broke the handle off the water pump to stop people getting their water from it."

"And did the disease clear up?"

"It did. And this proved a huge step forward in understanding how diseases spread. Nowadays I'm considered somewhat of pioneer in the science of the spread of infectious diseases." Dr Snow looked quietly proud of his work.

"So why didn't people listen to you earlier?" Claudia asked in frustration. "You were clearly right. If they had just followed what you were saying before, maybe even more lives would have been saved."

Claudia really wanted to know the answer to this question. She felt that if people would just listen to her then things would get done so much quicker. To her initial disappointment, Dr. Snow did not directly answer her question.

"I didn't just work on clearing up this disease though." He said instead. "My main job was to give people drugs that would mean they were not in pain when they are being operated on. I worked with a lot with women when they were giving birth to make sure they weren't in pain, I even helped Queen Victoria to give birth to two of her children."

Claudia was impressed. Dr Snow went on.

"In order to prevent pain I used to give patients a particular drug, a drug that doctors no longer use today. People always told me that it wasn't safe to use that drug and that I shouldn't be giving it to my patients. I knew better of course, I was absolutely convinced it was safe and they would all be well."

Dr. Snow paused for a few seconds. Claudia thought about what he was saying.

"You said that doctors no longer used this drug." She said trying to understand what he meant. "Was it not safe to use after all?"

"Oh it could be perfectly safe if used absolutely correctly." He replied "But...but if not used absolutely correctly..."

There was a pause. Dr. Snow was no longer proud of himself. He was now very unhappy.

"People died." He said eventually "That is why doctors no longer use this drug."

"So you were wrong about that drug?"

"I was wrong. I know that now but at the time I didn't listen to other people. And the reason why I didn't listen to other people about this drug is exactly the same reason why other people didn't listen to me about the disease. I was trying to do the right thing, I was sure I was doing the right thing and thought that I knew exactly what was correct and what wasn't correct."

Claudia thought more about what the man was telling her. She had receiving a lot of advice recently and was beginning to put it all together.

"Trying to understand things for yourself and solving all of the problems is very impressive." He went on "Having opinions on things is very important but it's easy to have an opinion. Literally anyone can have an opinion on any subject. What's hard is to listen carefully to other people and the hardest thing of all is admitting when you are wrong."

Chapter 14 College Green

"Lancelot Blackburne was Archbishop of York from 1724 until his death in 1743 and is known as The Pirate Bishop. He had spent his younger days in the Caribbean where he was paid handsomely for what is described as "secret services" for King Charles II. This has led to the rumour that he had been employed as a buccaneer, which was basically a pirate working for the King who would capture enemy ships and send the booty back to England. There is little clear evidence to confirm this for sure and he certainly did no pirating during his time in York, however he was well known for keeping up some of his earlier ways of drinking and poor behaviour. Those that knew him said that his behaviour was rarely up to the standard expected of an Archbishop and frequently not up the standard expected of a pirate."

Charles Wellbeloved's Encyclopaedia of All Things York, Page 243

*

The last person that Claudia thought would help her find a key was Mr Barry. Throughout all of her adventures in York Claudia had continued to attend her weekly piano lessons with Mr Barry down in St. Andrewgate. Claudia enjoyed playing the piano and liked her teacher who was always a bundle of energy and enthusiasm. The only problem was just that every lesson resulted in Mr Barry throwing several new pieces of music at Claudia for her to have to learn the following week. And every time they went through a new piece of music they always had to go through the same checklist.

"Now first things first, let's understand what the piece is." Mr Barry said as always "What time signature is it in?"

"3/4" Claudia replied

"Excellent. The word presto is written at the top here, what does that tell us?"

"That it should be played quickly?"

"Spot on. Ok, what key signature is it in?"

"G"

"How do you know it's a key of G?"

"Because it has an F-sharp in it but no other sharps or flats."

"Excellent, and can you find an F-sharp on the keyboard?"
Claudia put her hands over the three black keys towards the centre of the piano. A sharp, G sharp and F sharp. She pressed the key that was furthest to the left of these to indicate she had found the right note. Hang on, something was going on in her brain.

"And can you play a scale in G?" Mr Barry continued.

Claudia played the notes is a G scale, starting with the G before moving up to the A, B, C, D, E and making sure she played a F Sharp before playing G again and moving back down the scale to her starting position.

"Great. So we know it is in the key of G..." Mr Barry went on.

"Is there a key of A-sharp?" Claudia interrupted him.

Taken by surprise, Mr Barry had to think about it for a second.

"Yes, technically there is a key of A-sharp although people don't really use it." He finally said hesitantly

"Why not?" Claudia's mind was racing

"Because it contains things called double sharps which aren't really practical. People generally replace it with a key of B-flat which is in practice the same thing."

Claudia looked down at the keys, she pressed the white note that she knew was an A and then pressed the black note that was immediately to the right. This was the A-sharp. She then moved her fingers up to the next white note on the right. This was a B. She moved down to the black key again. Moving this way made the same black note a B-flat. A-sharp and B-flat were the same note. If she played a scale starting at A-sharp this would be the key of A-sharp. If she played a key starting at B flat, which was the same note, then this was a scale in the key of B-flat. And the two keys were the same.

"A sharp key, maybe too sharp or alternatively it may be flat." She said to herself

"I guess you could say that yes. It's an odd way to say anything but I guess it makes sense." Mr Barry was totally confused by what was happening. His bottom jaw hung slightly open and his eyes were slightly narrowed.

"Could I write down all of the notes in the B Flat key?" Claudia asked grabbing a pencil and piece of paper

"Certainly. The scale you need to play will go B flat, C, D, E flat, F, G, A and B flat again."

*

"PSSSSSSSST."

Claudia heard it but had no idea where it was coming from. She didn't even know if it was coming from her own world or from the Echo World. She wasn't entirely sure if she had definitely even heard it or if it was her imagination.

"PSSSSSSSSSSSSSSSSSSST."

There it was again. So it was definitely real. Now all she had to do was figure out where it was coming from. She was stood by College Green at the east end of The Minster with her mother. They had been here countless times before as he mother told her again and again about the how the Great East Window was the largest medieval stained glass window in the world. However she had never heard anyone try to get her attention before.

"PSSSSST. Hey you down there."

Claudia looked up. She assumed that it was her that was being summoned. The only thing she could see that could possibly have been speaking to her was a row of stone carved heads underneath the Great East Window. Well that answered which world this was coming from. She felt her own world dissolve away from her as she entered the Echo World.

"You there." One of the heads shouted at her.

She'd seen the heads many times before. They were all men, some bearded, some wearing hats. One even wore a crown. The head that had spoken to her was 2nd from the right, with a weather beaten face and wearing a cap that definitely made it look like he was from the Middle Ages.

"Hello." Claudia replied tentatively.

"Ah you can hear me then." The head went on "I was wondering."

"Yes, sorry. I could hear you, I just didn't know you were speaking to me."

"I wasn't really. Well not specifically speaking to you. I was just trying my luck with everyone down there."

"Oh."

Claudia was a bit put out. She was beginning to think that she was quite special and wasn't entirely sure how to take this news.

"I see you're admiring my cap?" The head continued. "I get to wear this because I was a Lord Mayor of York. Snazzy isn't it."

"You were a Mayor?" Claudia repeated

"LORD Mayor if you don't mind. Get it right."

"Sorry. So which Lord Mayor were you?"

"Errrm. I don't know really. Whichever Lord Mayor the stonemason who carved me was thinking of I suppose. I came out of his imagination but once he'd carved me I was here."

"So why did you want to speak to me.

"I just get a bit lonely up here." The Lord Mayor continued "And after hundreds of years on your own you get a bit desperate for company. Any company really."

"How could you be lonely?" Claudia asked "Surely you can just speak to one of the other heads."

"Well I could try The Bishop here"

The Lord Mayor turned to his left and started speaking to another head that was wearing a bishop's hat.

"YOUR GRACE." He shouted "YOUR GRACE. YOUR G.....deaf as a post. I SAID, YOUR GRACE."

"What?" The Bishop replied tetchily.

"HOW ARE YOU YOUR GRACE?"

"How far is my face?"

"Deaf as a post" The Lord Mayor grumbled again "I WAS ASKING IF YOU ARE WELL."

"Basking in a smell?"

"Why do I bother?" The Lord Mayor turned back to look down at Claudia "The worst thing is, he's got the youngest ears out of all of us."

Claudia looked along the row of heads again. Most looked like The Lord Mayor, stained and discoloured, the features of their face worn down or even in some cases missing entirely. In contrast The Bishop looked shiny and new, made from a light, cream coloured stone and all his features fully intact.

"Why is he so much younger than you?" Claudia asked The Lord Mayor.

"The modern day stonemasons down in their hut down there have given him a make complete makeover. Looks good doesn't he? Shame they couldn't fix his hearing."

"And what happened to the others?" Claudia asked further, pointing at older looking faces."

"Nothing more than countless years of facing up to whatever the British weather has to offer. Unlike the fancy Choir of Kings inside, we get no protection from the elements. Every time it rains, tiny amounts of us get washed away in the water. When the wind blows, small bits of grit get inside the dents in our face and roll around, eventually scouring out deep holes. And when you guys started burning coal all day every day, well it didn't do wonders for us put it that way. All that smoke making us dirty and what not. Not nice at all."

Claudia wished she hadn't asked. She wanted to move the conversation on.

"And the other faces. None of them talk to you?"

"Well most of them have their minds on more heavenly matters."

"Who are they?"

"Look at the face in the middle, does he look familiar? Long hair, a beard. Exactly the sort of face you see regularly on a church. He even has a halo. Do you recognise him?"

"Yes I think I do."

"And there are 6 faces either side of him that makes 12 friends in all. Does that sound familiar?"

"Twelve disciples yes."

"So between them you could say they make up a Choir of Heaven. But we're the Choir of Heaven and Earth so some of us have to be a bit more Earthly. So you've got me and The Bishop here at this end and then down the far end there is The King and The Master Mason."

Claudia looked down to the far end of the row of faces. The face at the far end was wearing a crown. That would make him The King then. But next to him...that didn't look right.

"There is a face missing." She said to The Lord Mayor. "Next to The King at the far end."

"Yes, that's where The Master Mason should be."

"So where is he?"

"No idea. We woke up one day and he was gone. I envy him really. Wherever he's gone, it has to be better than waiting around here day after day. But hang on...this looks promising. The sun's coming out."

Claudia hadn't even realised it had been a cloudy day until The Lord Mayor had drawn attention to it. Sure enough, as she looked up the thick layer of grey cloud began to part and the sun shine hit the stone walls of The Minster. She couldn't help but think to herself how much better it looked, how much better everything looked with the sun shining. Colours were lighter, reflections brighter. The contrast between the shadows and the light was stronger. The row of faces obviously approved as well. There was movement as if they were coming alive, blinking in the sun, taking strength from the energy of the warm rays. She felt like she was about to hear why they were called The Choir of Heaven and Earth. Yes indeed, here came the song.

We've waited on this church for all these years

We face up to every challenge offered

Put up with wears and tears and fears and tears

So no one knows quite just how much we've suffered

The rain may only fall in drops and drips

But slowly will we all be washed away

The winds will scour, our features will be stripped

Our nose, our ears get smaller every day

But now the sun breaks out and clears the skies

We bask and glow within its warm embrace

We shine so bright to dazzle all your eyes

As rays light up each hand carved handsome face

Each time the sun ensures a fresh rebirth

We sing once more, The Choir of Heaven and Earth

The choir was correct, everything was better in the sunshine, even autumnal sunshine late in the year. Buildings were lit up in their full glory, stone looked lighter and creamier, glass glistened and people smiled. Claudia no longer cared that Balthazar was adamant that the silver key had nothing to do with St. William, she felt confident and happy and was just going to go for it. Her thoughts also went back to some of the advice she had received recently. Don't be afraid of the uncertainty of fog, never wait for other people to do things for you, always listen to other people and always accept that sometimes you might be wrong.

She walked the short distance between the Great East Window and St. William's College, stood in front of the heavy wooden door and looked up to the half metre high carving above the entrance. St. William was sat in the same pose as he always was, holding a crook with his left hand and lifting his right hand up with fingers raised in order to give a blessing to anybody who happened to be passing by. To his left was the coat of arms of York Minster, complete with a set of crossed silver keys. She could be wrong but it was worth a try. Claudia Ding cleared her throat and began to speak.

"Excuse me .. erm ....Your Grace"

She winced, not knowing if Your Grace was what the correct way to address a Saint. Maybe it was, although it didn't sound right. She tried again.

"Excuse me Your Holy Saintness"

Whatever the correct way to address a Saint, it certainly wasn't that. She pretended it hadn't just happened and continued anyway.

"I was wondering, if it was possible, could I please borrow the silver Peterkey. Please. I really would be most grateful. Thank you kindly."

She closed her eyes, slightly ashamed that she was even trying this.

"Yes of course you can." Replied the carving.

Claudia opened her eyes in surprise. She looked carefully at the carving, half expecting to find that she had imagined it speaking. But no, it had definitely moved.

"Are you sure?" She asked nervously.

"I've been waiting for a long time for someone to come and ask politely for this key." St. William continued. "And you did ask so politely. But first...."

Oh dear, this didn't sound so promising.

"...but first. Could you tell me who the Five Sisters are?"
"The Five Sisters?" Claudia repeated

"Yes the Five Sisters. It's not much to ask. I just couldn't give this key to someone who didn't know who they were. If you want to find them, I suggest looking near to the heart and the rose."

Great, just after she thought she'd solved one of the map's clues she gets another problem set for her. Well these things aren't meant to be easy are they?

Chapter 15 King's Manor

Mathilda was worried. She was worried about her young friend Claudia Ding. Actually she was worried about an awful lot of things at the moment. She still wasn't sure why she had been captured or why she was being held here. She was worried about the man who had been put in there with her, he seemed in a particularly bad way. But it was Claudia she was worried about right now, what was she up to? Was she safe? Was she looking for her? Was anybody going to come and help? There was a lot on her mind.

*

Whoever or wherever the Five Sisters were, Claudia had been told to look near the heart and the rose. Something had clicked in her mind, she wasn't sure what it was but she knew that she had thought about both hearts and roses when she had gone out to visit Etty the Artist in Exhibition Square. She didn't know what she might find out there but it was worth a visit, she might come up with the answer.

Claudia stood in Exhibition Square and thought hard. Hearts and roses. Roses and hearts. What was the link? Then she remembered the flowers on the extravagant carving above the door in King's Manor. Well that was a good place to start at least.

Queen Catherine wasn't in the gardens of King's Manor this time. The only person about was a man on a ladder who appeared to be painting the carving above the door.

"Hello there" Claudia said nervously.

There was no answer.

"Hello there." Claudia said again

"He won't answer you"

Claudia almost jumped out of her skin. She turned around to see two men stood behind her. Both men had dark hair and pointy beards and were wearing black capes and tall hats.

"We've been trying to get him to talk for hundreds of years." Said one of the men "but he won't answer. It's a shame because if he could speak he'd be able to settle an argument we've been having."

"And who are you?" Claudia asked. She realised as she was speaking that she probably sounded a bit rude but she was still getting over the shock.

"Oh of course, how impolite of us." The man replied with a smile "Allow me to introduce myself. My name is Sir Thomas Fairfax and it is the greatest pleasure to make your acquaintance." He made an elaborate bow towards Claudia.

"And my name is Sir Thomas Herbert." The other man said with an equally elaborate bow. "And I am your most humble and obedient servant."

"Not at all good sirs." Claudia replied enjoying herself in copying their gentlemanly manners. "My name is Claudia Ding and I assure you that the pleasure is mine and mine alone."

She bowed back to them getting as low as possible. The three of them stood for a few seconds all in the same bowing stance. Claudia realised that if she didn't say something they may stay like that forever. She straightened herself up and looked around for something to say.

"So this carving" she asked hesitantly "What is it?"

Fairfax and Herbert both straightened themselves back up and looked at her.

"That is the Coat of Arms of a King." Fairfax answered her.

"Particularly Coat of Arms of King Charles the First." Herbert continued. "You can tell it is for King Charles if you look towards the top either side of the gold crown you'll see the letters C and R. Now C, as might guess, stands for Charles and R stands for Rex which is the Latin word for king."

"King Charles the First" Repeated Claudia in thought "So how old is it?"

"Coming up to 400 years old." Fairfax replied "But it does sometimes get repainted to keep it looking fresh."

"400 years old. Wow that's impressive." Claudia wasn't lying, she was genuinely impressed. "But what does it mean."

Fairfax and Herbert looked at each, Fairfax took a deep breath as if he was going to take responsibility to explain it to her and Herbert nodded his approval.

"The Coat of Arms is essentially a king showing off how powerful he is. You'll see there are several symbols all indicating that Charles was King of England. There is the large gold lion holding an English flag along with other sets of smaller gold lions of red backgrounds and those red flowers around there which are actually roses."

Claudia had heard the word roses but didn't have time to ask for more information because Fairfax was still going.

"There's also the unicorn holding a Scottish flag, there's a red lion and those blue flowers are Scottish thistles. These all indicate that he was also King of the Scots. His father James had been the first person to be both King of England and King of the Scots. What's more, he is also claiming to be King of Ireland, you can tell because there is that gold harp on a blue background. But he goes even further than that, can you see those gold lilies on a blue background. They are called the Fleur de Lis and they are there because King Charles is claiming that he is also the true and rightful King of France."

"King of France." Claudia said in shock.

"Yes. For 500 years the monarchs of this country claimed that they were also the true rightful King of France."

"What did the actual King of France think about that?" Claudia asked in confusion.

"Well they always disagreed." Fairfax was grinning as he spoke now "But you know what the French are like, they argue over everything."

"This was not unusual." Herbert intervened "One king would marry another king's daughter or another king's sister and so their children would have a claim to both crowns. After a while these claims would add up and a king would sit there claiming that he was the rightful ruler of every country he could see."

Claudia was impressed. She wanted to go back and discuss what she'd heard. Particularly the roses but also she knew that King Charles was important but she could not remember why. However, it was clear that there was more information coming her way and it was now Herbert's turn to explain it to her.

"There are also two royal mottos. One originally adopted in the 14th Century by King Edward III that is written on the blue garter around the centre of the carving. It says *Honi Soit Qui Mal Y Pense* which means something like *Shame on Him Who Thinks Evil* or basically it is a bad thing to think badly of something. Then there is another motto written along the bottom, a motto adopted in the 15th Century by Henry V which says *Dieu Et Mon Droit* which translates to *God and My Right*.

"His right what? Right arm? Right foot?" Claudia asked

"His right to rule. God had appointed him king and nobody had any authority over him. Our King Charles took this divine right to rule very seriously. Members of Parliament believed that as representatives of the people of the country, they should have say in how the country should be run but the king ignored them and refused to work with them."

"Ooo...ooo...ooo" Claudia was excited, she finally remembered why she knew about King Charles "I know this. The King and Parliament had a long war didn't they? The Civil War it's called isn't it. Roundheads versus Cavaliers and all that. That must have been very exciting."

"There was nothing exciting about the war." Fairfax replied solemnly "Battles right the way across England and Scotland, terrible violence in Ireland, death, destruction, disease, and families torn apart. Nothing exciting at all."

"Yes, sorry." Claudia felt embarrassed by her misplaced enthusiasm. "Were you part of the war?"

"I certainly was." Fairfax went on "I did not want to be part of that or any other war but King Charles left us with absolutely no choice. He ignored parliament, ignored the people and tried to rule the country as if it was his and his alone. We tried everything in our powers to get him to co-operate but he refused point blank and left us with no choice but to go to war against him and his supporters. I was a commander in the Parliament Army that laid siege to this City of York in 1644. There were around 20,000 of us attacking with our guns, canons and barrels gunpowder and around 5,000 soldiers loyal to the King on the inside of the city trying to keep us out."

"Well you would have got in fairly easily then. You seemed to have the dominant army."

"You'd think so. But those blasted city walls over there proved too strong for us." Fairfax gestured angrily towards Bootham Bar and the city walls. "For three months we attacked and even with all of our canons we still couldn't get through. It was only after the King's Army lost a large battle nearby that they abandoned York and were able to come in and capture the city."

"Was it important to capture York?"

"Absolutely vital. Right the way from Roman times onwards, if you can control York then you control the entire of the North of England. And I also personally love the city where I used to spend a lot of time and was in great admiration of its fascinating history and wonderful buildings. When we were attacking the city I made absolutely sure that none of our canons would damage any of the old churches that were here. Even then I had to ban men form our own army from going into The Minster and smashing all the stained glass windows in there."

"Why on earth would they do that?" Claudia asked in surprise.

"They thought they were doing the right thing. Lots of people at this time thought that churches had become far too full of distractions. They thought that to create a purer, better church they would have to destroy any stained glass windows, statues, paintings and the like so that all that remained was you and God."

"Well it's a good job you stopped them."

"I managed to stop them here but many churches and cathedrals around the country didn't manage to stop people. In fact, so many windows were smashed at this time that York Minster now contains more than half of the original, authentic medieval stained glass in England. It's easy to judge people but as I say, they really did think they were doing the right thing."

"So what happened next, with the war?"

"Myself and another of the commanders here called Oliver Cromwell..."

"Oh I definitely heard of him" Claudia interrupted all proud of herself again

"Yes, well Cromwell and I were later put in charge in running all of Parliament's Army. Gradually we managed to win enough battles to win the war and King Charles was captured and imprisoned."

"And what happened to him?" Claudia had a suspicion it did not end well for Charles.

"By then Cromwell and his supporters were beginning to take control. They blamed King Charles for the entire war, claiming that without him there would have been no fighting, no deaths and no destruction. They felt that as long as he refused to acknowledge Parliament's authority then the only solution would be to execute him as a traitor. I completely disagreed with this, I thought that executing him would be a mistake. In fact my wife was even thrown out of the King's trial because she was objecting so loudly. However by then, Cromwell had well and truly won. And that's when Sir Thomas Herbert here comes into the story."

"Indeed I do." Herbert took up the tale. "I was a supporter of Parliament but when the King was imprisoned I was tasked with looking after him. When he was sentenced to death I was with him and was able to look after him in his final days. Even though I disagreed with him and believed that Parliament was correct to fight against him, I realised that in the end he was just a man. Just a man facing up to his death who needed kindness and support. I was even with him on the night before his execution."

"Wasn't Cromwell then put in charge of the country?" Claudia asked again

"He was." Herbert replied "Most of the moderate people like Fairfax here retired and went to live in the country and Cromwell and his Puritan supporters ran the country for about ten years."

"But after Cromwell died" Fairfax jumped in "Most of us decided that we had been better off with a king as long as that king would always promise to work with Parliament in a way that King Charles I would not do. So I went to speak to the old King's son, offered him the throne and he became King Charles II. And we've kept our monarchs to this day."

"The new King recognised the kindness I had shown his father" Herbert now continued "He gave me a reward and a title and I retired back here to York, where I had been born, and lived out my days in this wonderful city."

"So what about this Coat of Arms. What's the mystery that you want clearing up?" Claudia asked

"Look again at the motto along the bottom." Herbert instructed "Do you seen anything odd?"

"Dieu Et Mon Droit." Claudia read slowly "The N. The N in Mon is written back to front. Should it be written like that?"

"No." Fairfax said with a smile "It's never written like that anywhere else. That's the mystery. I think it's nothing but a mistake. I think that the person who carved it may well have been unable to read or write. He was simply just asked to copy something and didn't now he was doing it wrong."

"And I think it must be deliberate." Herbert responded "I think you'd never go to all that trouble of carving all of that and leave in such a silly mistake. I think this was deliberately put in as a message to King Charles. Even if you have *Mon Droit*, even if you have a divine right to rule, you can still make mistakes. I believe someone is reminding him that nobody is perfect."

"Unfortunately." Fairfax jumped in again "Unless we can speak to the people who originally carved it, we'll never know the answer to this mystery. And this guy is not speaking."

Chapter 16 Dean's Park

Meg Montgomery was worried. She was worried about lots of things of course but right now she was most worried about her brother Gus. How long could it take anybody to simply go from The Shambles to York Minster and back? Certainly not the couple of hours he'd taken. Finally the door opened and Gus came sloping into the shop.

"Hi Meg, I'm back"

"About time, what took you?"

"Oh yes, sorry about that. I bumped into the echo of a group of American tourists being shown around The Minster. They were a nice bunch, they came from *New* York. And we got chatting about how different New York is from, well Old York? York? What would you call it."

"York of course. Same thing as you'd call it if you were speaking to anybody else."

"Yes I suppose you're right. But anyway, as I say we got chatting and I ended up kind of joining in the tour. We went up the central tower, it's a long way up there."

"I know it is, and looking at that ever expanding belly of yours, I'm pretty surprised you made it all the way up. Isn't it something like 275 steps up there? You've never walked 275 steps anywhere."

"Well it was a bit of a struggle so I actually got one of the Americans to give me a piggy back. It took us a while but she got us up in the end."

"You didn't' really did you...Oh I see, very good. There's no need to smirk like that."

Gus did seem pleased to get one over his sister for once.

"Right well back to important things" She continued quickly "You went to The Minster for a purpose. Was she there?"

"Yes she was."

"And did you speak to her."

"Yes of course."

"So what did she say?"

*

Claudia had left King's Manor and was heading back towards The Minster area. She knew exactly where to find the heart and the rose and it had nothing to do with the carving above the door.

She thought about what Sir Thomas Fairfax had told her about the men who wanted to smash the stained glass windows in The Minster. They may well have thought that would have been doing the correct thing but it would have been a real shame to lose such lovely and impressive things. The window that was staring at her at the moment was the large window at the west end of the giant cross that made up the building. There in the middle of the window, traced out in the stonework was what looked just like a huge heart. The Heart of Yorkshire this was called. She also knew that if she went around to the south end of the cross there would be a circular window known as the Rose Window filled with the red and white roses that celebrated the marriage of Queen Catherine's husband's parents. That was a heart and a rose sorted so the Five Sisters must be somewhere around her. The window at the east of the cross she had seen many times before of course, her mother never failed to take the opportunity to call the Great East Window the largest mediaeval stained glass window in the world. That meant that she needed to look at the north end of the cross.

Claudia made her way through the grassy area immediately north of The Minster known as Dean's Park. Walking along the length of The Minster she once more marvelled at the sheer size of the thing. Her mother had told her it had taken 250 years to build and from this angle she could see why. How many people did it take to build it? How much did it cost? It must have been a fortune.

She reached the arm of the cross that was projecting northwards and stopped to look at it. It was dominated by 5 tall and thin windows. The windows here were different to the other grand windows she had seen. They looked thinner, pointier, darker and somehow older. The Great East Window for example was a single expanse of window 10 metres wide and 25 metres broken up by stone and lead tracings to make hundreds of small panels. On the north side there was these 5 separate windows, each maybe only 1 metre across and around 15 metres high. These must be the Five Sisters. What a clever girl she was.

*

"I never saw them of course, any of them" St. William said sadly after Claudia had told him she had found the Five Sisters and the other windows in the building.

"Why not?" She asked curiously.

"Because this building wasn't started until after I had died. I was Archbishop of York in the 1140's and 1150's and this building and all of the windows in it were not begun until 1220. There was a cathedral already on this spot in my time, it was large and impressive in its own way but not nearly as big as the current building. I was popular and respected but some people feared my popularity. In fact, I may even have been murdered when a rival priest put poison in my cup. I was later made a saint in 1227. Just 7 years after they had started to rebuild this wonderful cathedral. Having a saint buried here was really useful as pilgrims would come and pay the church money to be allowed to pray at my tomb here. You could say that I helped build The Minster. However, I would have loved to see the completed building when I was still alive. Here, you've deserved this."

He reached out towards the shield on his left and grabbed something. To Claudia's surprise, one of the keys that had seemed to be a flat 2 dimensional painting had become a fully functioning 3 dimensional key sat in St. William's hand. He lent forward and passed the key over to Claudia.

"Thank you very much … erm … your excellency." She stammered nervously

"Don't mention it at all. Good luck young lady, whatever your plans." The carving of St William replied before returning to its original position and freezing in place.

Well that was surprisingly easy. She should have trusted her instincts from the start. She always knew she should have been talking to St William. Why didn't people listen to her more often?

Now for the next step. There was loud organ music coming from inside The Minster. Time to investigate.

Claudia entered York Minster by the doors at the west end. The building may have been impressively large from the outside but once again she was blown away by huge, cavernous space in the empty cathedral. With no other visible people in there, the only thing filling the void was the music. Individual notes were bouncing around off walls and windows, hitting into to each other and joining together to create new chords. Claudia looked up and marvelled at everything that was in there. If she had the time she could stay here all day but she had someone to try and find.

Claudia moved through the building and walked to the left of the organ. There was a figure sat in the shadows, exactly as she was hoping there would be. She let her eyes adjust to the low light and studied the person carefully. It was definitely the same lady as before still wearing her rich velvet cloak and white veil.

"Excuse me Queen Philippa." She said as politely as possible "Could I sit down here?"

"Of course you can my dear" Queen Philippa said, looking her way with a smile "It is nice to see you again."

Claudia felt good. Things were going well for her today.

"So how did you find out my name?" Queen Philippa asked.

"I spoke to my mother and she said something that … erm …"

Claudia felt her voice trailing under the withering look of Queen Philippa.

"Is the same mother that never has any time for you?" The Queen asked slyly

"I suppose so yes."

There was another short silence as Claudia felt slightly ashamed of herself. She wanted to move the conversation on to something new.

"Is your husband one of the Stone Carved Choir of Kings?" She asked feeling this was safe territory.

"Yes he is. King Edward III, stood proudly and defiantly with the others." Queen Philippa replied.

"They say they'll come to the aid of anybody in need."

"That's what they say. Not all Kings are grand, impressive people in their own lifetime of course. Some of them are pretty useless. In fact both my Father-in-Law Edward II and my Grandson Richard II were forced to stand down and let someone else take over as king. But these statues, they were carved with respect and affection. They have stood here as a symbol of hope and loyalty for the people of York to look up to and admire. I am sure that they are genuine when they say that want to aid those that need help and I shall make sure that they come to your aid if you ever require them."

Claudia believed the Queen when she said this. If anybody could make something like that happen, Philippa of Hainault was that person.

"It's important to have good thoughts about people isn't it" Claudia said trying to impress the Queen. "Shame on him who thinks evil."

"Honi Soit Qui Mal Y Pense." Queen Philippa replied "My husband would be proud of you.

"You and your husband had children didn't you?" Claudia asked "How many children did you have?"

"Thirteen." Queen Philippa replied.

Claudia was impressed. That was a lot of children. Well done her.

"Did you say that some of them were Dukes?"
"Yes, there were 5 Dukes and 2 Countesses."
Claudia added up the numbers. That didn't come to thirteen children.

"So what about the rest of them?" She asked.

There was no reply. Instead, Queen Philippa looked forward mournfully and respectfully lowered her eyes. Claudia looked forward as well to see what the Queen might have been looking at. She knew that this part of the building was lined with tombs and monuments but she hadn't thought to look at them in any detail. Claudia took a good look at the tomb straight in front of them. Like many other tombs, lying on top there was a life size depiction of the person who was laid at rest inside. This particular carving was of a child. A boy, maybe ten years old or so and laying down as if asleep. There was writing below the tomb.

Prince William of Hatfield

Second son of King Edward III and Queen Philippa: Younger brother of the Black Prince. Died as a child.

Claudia realised that she could be an idiot. She could not have been more wrong about this woman who she thought was suspiciously hiding in the shadows. She wasn't hiding there at all, she was simply trying to mourn the loss of her child. Claudia admonished herself for not looking round more carefully before? It would have been so easy to work all of this out by simply being more observant. Dr. Snow had been correct, she'd been so sure that Philippa was the Queen of Shadows that she didn't even consider that she might have got it wrong.

"He didn't look like that." Queen Philippa said gesturing towards the tomb. "He never had a chance to look like that. He was never a child. He was a baby, not even six months old. Other people thought it wouldn't be dignified to have a statue of a baby on a tomb so they persuaded me that he should be depicted as a child. But this isn't what he looked like. I should never have let them talk me into that. It doesn't matter how long ago it was or how many other children you have, it never stops hurting"

Queen Philippa turned to look straight at Claudia.

"Now if I'm not mistaken" she continued with a kindly smile forcing its way onto her face "You've come to collect the gold Peterkey."

"How did you know I was searching for the key?" Claudia asked Queen Philippa

"Why else would you come in here again? It's certainly not to speak to an old lady like me." The Queen replied

"So you know how to find it?"

"Well I couldn't tell you that of course. However, I've sat here for many years waiting for someone to play a certain combination of notes on that organ but as yet no one has. I have a feeling that today is going to be different."

The two of them looked towards the giant organ, sitting right at the centre of the building and playing a constant soothing beat as if it was the heart of the cathedral.

"Go on Claudia" Philippa said encouragingly "You know what to do."

Claudia nodded and walked over to the steps to the organ. She stopped at the bottom for a while in order to build her confidence. She looked back towards the powerful figure of Queen Philippa as if to gain permission climb the steps, Philippa nodded and smiled and Claudia began to climb the steps.

As she climbed the steps to the organ the music began to fade, slowly and gradually getting quieter and quieter until dying out entirely as she reached the top of the steps. Claudia sat down at the keyboard and looked down in amazement. This was nothing like the small piano she played at Mr Barry's house or the electric keyboard she had at home to practice on. There were piano keys everywhere, several rows of black and white keys looking up at her expectantly surrounded by all sorts of switches and stops. She took out the piece of paper she had written down the B-flat scale on and scanned the keyboard. All she needed was to start was to find a B-flat, there were several to choose from so she picked one at random and pressed it carefully, the sound of the note filled the empty cathedral giving Claudia an immense sense of power, she moved up to the C above it and enjoyed the change in tone as it came out of the organ pipes. She moved up the scale to the D, then E-flat, F, G, A and finally B-flat again. As she pressed the final note she heard a distinct click come from below the keyboard and small draw opened very slightly. The drawer wasn't open enough to get inside it but she could see there was definitely something in there. Claudia had a thought and deliberately played a note that wasn't in the key of B-flat, choosing to play an F sharp. As she suspected, the draw slammed shut and another loud click told her it was locked shut. Claudia chose another B-flat to start with, quickly played a scale and to her delight the draw partially opened again. She chose another B-flat to start with and played another scale and the drawer opened up slightly more, not enough to get inside but open enough for Claudia to see the thing inside was glistening in the light. Another B-flat scale and the draw opened up slightly more, one more B-flat scale and the drawer opened up fully. Claudia, reached in and pulled out a shiny golden key.

She had done it, she had found all four of the Peterkeys. She should have been absolutely delighted, completely over the moon with pride at her achievement but she couldn't get carried away. She had the keys but what good were they, Mathilda was still missing and may still be in danger and she had no idea how the keys were going to help at all.

Chapter 17 Castlegate

"There is no doubt about it of course, York is simply a very foggy city. The resource rich hills that surround the city don't just drain rivers down into the flat land in the middle, cold dense air flows downwards as well and pools in the Vale of York with nowhere to go but to condense into mist. The residents of the city regularly wake up to find themselves blanketed in a layer of fog and sometimes find it still there when they go to bed again at the end of the day. Fog needs to be respected of course but not feared, it just adds to the look of the place with old streets and buildings emerging from the mist like ghosts from the past. Yes, there is no doubt that York is a very foggy city. A beautiful, foggy wonderful city."

Charles Wellbeloved's Encyclopaedia of All Things York, Page 115

*

Claudia and her mother stepped off the 415 bus and moved amongst the crowded hordes of Saturday morning shoppers.

"Bank, lecture at the library, piano lesson, shopping." Her mother barked the order of the day at her.

"Finding and freeing my friend Mathilda." Claudia whispered to herself

"What's that honey?"

"Oh nothing."

How was she going to find Mathilda? It was still a deep mystery to her. She had found all four Peterkeys but had no idea at all how to use them.

She felt one of the other shoppers bumping into her, a gruff voice muttered an apology and a piece of paper was thrust into her hand.

"Watch where you're going Claudia." Her mother said.

It was just like her mother to blame Claudia for someone else bumping into her but she had bigger things to worry about right now. She was desperately looking around for the man who had given her the piece of paper, but he'd disappeared into the crowd. Or maybe disappeared altogether.

Claudia kept the piece of paper tight in her pocket until she was sat alone in the library and was sure no one was watching her. She opened it up and read what was written.

Claudia,

I hope you get this note. I still need your help. I'm in a prison cell in York Castle. I can't tell you anymore. Come and find me.

Come quickly

Mathilda

Claudia knew immediately where she needed to go. The old prison cells at York Castle Museum may still hold a terror over her but she had no choice but go and confront her fears. She needed some support. There was only one friend she could trust.

"I need your help." Claudia said in as firm and calm manner as she could manage "You are my best friend in this world and the only one I can truly trust. What do you say Stonecat, will you help me?"

There was a silence as the two of them looked at each. Claudia did not know what Stonecat was going to say but she was sure that he wanted to help.

"It's not in a cat's nature to help." Came the eventual reply "We tend to look out for ourselves."

Stonecat remained resolutely on his ledge above the doorway, looking down on Claudia with a serious face.

"I know that Stonecat." Claudia went on "But I also know that deep down you really want to help and that you have been speaking to other cats who may also come to the rescue."

"I don't really speak to other cats. I like to keep to myself." Stonecat said looking away from her.

Claudia was frustrated. She knew Stonecat was being awkward but she didn't want to push him.

"OK. If that is how you feel then I won't argue. But if you do change your mind then I am going down to the Castle. Any help you can give, anything at all, would be gratefully received."

"If you say so" Stonecat settled down as if going to sleep and turned his back on her completely.

This was not good, she was going to have to do this alone.

Claudia made her way slowly down towards the castle, first walking down Stonegate and then heading down Davygate and Parliament Street. She was used to this being a wide and busy shopping but right now it was almost entirely empty with just a handful of other bodies in sight. On the left hand side of the road a group of women in cheap Victorian dresses shared a joke over a cup of tea and portion of fish and chips whilst further down a man in First World War Army uniform was chatting to a priest.

Claudia wasn't sure if they were watching her or even if they could see her. At this moment in time she didn't really know what to believe.

At the end of Parliament Street she turned right onto Coppergate then finally onto Castlegate. The imposing sight of Clifford's Tower rose into view and she felt her heart rate increasing as she walked past the tower perched high on its hill and made her way towards York Castle Museum.

She walked through the main entrance and looked around. It looked so different to what she was used to, no staff, no visitors, no café, not even the gift shop. Struggling to keep her breath under control she made her way down to the 18th Century prison cells. They were just like she had remembered; dark, cramped and eerie. The stone walls echoed with her footsteps and the small, barred windows barely let any light in at all. She felt trapped and threatened and didn't want to spend any time here at all.

"Hello" She called out nervously "Mathilda. Can you hear me? Are you there?"

"Claudia?"

The reply filled her with joy.

"Claudia is that you?"

It was definitely Mathilda's voice she could hear. She followed the voice to a closed doorway of one of the dank and dreary cells.

Up against the barred windows on the door a cell was a familiar sight. Mathilda's face looked dirty, her long black hair was straggly and she looked thinner than Claudia remembered.

"Oh Claudia you clever, clever girl" Mathilda called out "I knew you were special. But how on earth did you find us?"

"What do you mean us?" Claudia asked in confusion.

Mathilda moved away from the window and allowed Claudia a clear view inside. There was a man sat on the floor of the cell behind her. He was wearing a cap and clothes very similar to The Lord Mayor she had met at The Choir of Heaven and Earth. At one point his clothes may have been quite grand and luxurious but right now they looked tattered and torn. He was slumped over with his face away from the door but Claudia suspected he might be crying.

"It's alright Master Mason." Mathilda said in a soothing manner "My friend has come to save us."

"I don't deserve saving" The Master Mason replied softly. He sounded desperate.

This was the Master Mason then, one of the other members of The Choir of Heaven and Earth who had gone missing. He was no longer a stone carved head though, now he was fully formed in flesh and blood. One of the many inexplicable things in this world that Claudia did not understand.

Mathilda turned back to face Claudia

"But however did you find us here?" She asked again.

"I got your letters of course." Claudia replied

"What letters?"

"The letters telling me about the Queen of Shadows, about the Peterkeys and about how you were stuck in this prison cell."

"I didn't send you any letters." Mathilda crumpled up her forehead in confusion.

"So who did?"

"I told you not to trust anyone." A voice behind Claudia boomed out "I told you to not even trust your best friend."

Claudia turned to see where the voice was coming from. She knew exactly who she would see and it came as no surprise to her at all to find herself looking on the long face, silver hair and snow white flowing robes of Balthazar.

"Now you still have the remaining two keys that I need." He said in a calm clear voice. "Hand over the gold and silver keys."

"I don't have them." Claudia tried desperately to bluff her way out of danger.

"Yes you do." Balthazar was having none of her lies "Hand them over."

"I honestly don't have them." She tried once more.

"Yes you DO."

This was a new voice coming out of the darkness. The voice was louder, higher and far more terrifying than Balthazar's.

"HAND OVER THE KEYS."

The soundwaves of new voice smashed against the stone walls of the prison cells, echoing and bouncing around the small space before hitting Claudia's ears from all different directions.

"HAND OVER THE KEYS NOW."

She could finally see where the voice was coming from. Balthazar may have lied to her, tricked her and let her down but in one respect he had been completely honest. As soon as Claudia laid eyes on The Queen of Shadows then she knew exactly who she was looking at.

The Queen of Shadows wore long black clothes that seemed to form a fog around her so that she appeared not so much to be walking as floating towards them. As she moved, she seemed to suck all of the light out of everything she went past. There was not much light down here at the best of times but the blackness that fanned out from her and followed her around took darkness to another level. All around her the shadows and darkness seemed to swirl and move and Claudia was sure she could hear voices, very feint but whispering and muttering in the shadows. And yet, in amongst the darkness was a face which although cold and lifeless was shining a brilliant white light. Claudia felt her self looking away from The Queen of Shadows' face and meekly holding out the two keys in case the light coming towards her burned her eyes.

"I told you she'd find what we needed." Balthazar said to The Queen of Shadows once he was holding all four keys.

"You have done well Balthazar." She replied "And you will be well rewarded for your work."

"And what about us" Claudia asked in as defiant a manner as she could muster. She didn't sound very convincing.

"You three will be punished."

"Why?"

"Because I said so." The Queen of Shadows said without emotion "And because you have dared to try and thwart The Queen of Shadows."

"Who are you?" Mathilda asked in as strong a voice as she could muster. Mathilda didn't sound much more convincing than Claudia had done.

"I am the echo of every dark thought in the history of York. Every time someone has been angry, scared or jealous of other people then they have made me stronger. If you've ever behaved in a selfish way, if you've ever lost your temper with someone else or if you've ever felt unhappy then you have helped me grow."

"And why should you have the keys?" Mathilda tried again.

"Because I am the only one who can fully restore this city to its proper glory." The Queen of Shadows replied. "There are too many people polluting and downgrading the Echoes of York. They are taking away their sacredness from those of us who can truly appreciate them. I am the one who needs to control the incoming and outgoing of York because I am The Queen of Shadows and I know all."

Claudia tried one more time to argue with The Queen of Shadows and remembered some advice she had received recently.

"Aren't you willing to listen to other people?" She said "Maybe you'll find out you were wrong."

Claudia winced as she said it, worried that The Queen of Shadows would lose her temper. But she didn't. In fact, she didn't show any emotion at all.

"I am The Queen of Shadows." Was all she said "I know everything."

"But…" Claudia still tried more.

"Enough of this questioning"

The Queen of Shadows waved her hands and the Whispering Shadows that surrounded her flooded towards Claudia. The voices that she had heard in the background grew stronger and louder. Claudia could now make out what they were saying.

"You're stupid."

"You're useless."

"I hate you."

Claudia felt overwhelmed by the darkness and anger and shrank away from The Queen of Shadows. She wasn't going to be able to fight this battle, it was too much.

Chapter 18 Clifford's Tower

Claudia, Mathilda and The Master Mason were led from their prison cell, out of the building and towards Clifford's Tower. The Whispering Shadows swirled round them, muttering bad things and keeping the three of them in check.

"Where are you taking us?" Mathilda demanded.

"You will find out soon enough." Balthazar replied "Although I think The Master Mason knows what is going to happen."

"I'm sorry." Was all The Master Mason could reply before looking down at the ground meekly.

They were marched up to the base of Clifford's Tower. Claudia looked upwards, the hill on which they tower stood suddenly looked so much steeper and higher than it ever had before. The tower itself looked pretty imposing. It was not a large building, a square shape with rounded corners maybe 25 metres across and 15 metres high, but it had such thick and sturdy walls that Claudia wondered if it was place you could ever get out of if you were locked inside.

"Up the steps please" Balthazar ordered.

He remained calm and steady and in his voice and manner but Claudia felt that she didn't want to argue with him. The three captives and their two captors climbed the steps up to the tower entrance and moved inside the building. It was different to any other time she had been inside the tower, the floor had been dug up and a large pit had been put in.

"Down you go" Balthazar spoke again pointing towards a rope ladder that was hanging down one side of the pit.

"You don't have to do this to us." Mathilda tried her best "Please listen to us."

"I don't need to listen to anybody." The Queen of Shadows replied without emotion.

The three captives climbed down the ladder and Balthazar pulled it up after them. There was no way out from the pit now.

"This is our goodbyes then." The Queen of Shadows said "I expect we'll see you again. I doubt you'll see us though. The Mason will let you know what happens next, for the other two of you it will be a nice surprise."

Balthazar and The Queen of Shadows left the tower, The Queen of Shadows apparently floating away from them rather than walking.

Claudia gave a good look around. The top of the pit was considerably out of reach and the side of the pit was a smooth wall that didn't look like they could ever climb up get out. Around the pit, near the top of the walls, were a series of intricate carvings. They looked a lot like the grotesque Claudia had seen with her mother, only much more ugly and twisted. The figures were of faces or upper bodies of men and women but they all looked in tremendous pain. Their faces were twisted in agony and some of the carvings had visible wounds, sores or growths all over their faces and bodies. There was something else carved onto the sides of the pit, running between the grotesques. Claudia looked closely and realised that they were snakes. The snakes were crawling along the wall from carving to carving, rolling over one another. Some snakes were long and some sort, some with mouths shut and some with their fangs bared. The whole effect scared Claudia immensely. They must have taken a huge amount of skill to carve and Claudia now realised why The Queen of Shadows would need the Master Mason. He had presumably done all of this carving by himself.

"Right, we need to get out of here." Mathilda said determinedly

"It's no use." The Master Mason replied. "You'll never get out."

"Well I'm going to try anyway" She said running towards the edge of the pit.

Mathilda jumped as high as she could, trying to grab hold of one of the grotesques in an attempt to pull herself up. The carving she tried to grab was the head and upper body of a man who had apparently lost an eye. To her surprise, the grotesque slapped her hand away before she could find a hold. She jumped again and once more the grotesque reached out and slapped her away.

"You shouldn't have done that." The Master Mason said with alarm.

The grotesque that had slapped Mathilda began to let out a huge wail as if in great pain. All around him the other grotesques began crying in sympathy, wretchedly sobbing and flailing their arms or clutching their injuries. The noise might have been deafening and terrifying in its own right but Claudia noticed something much worse was happening.

The snakes had begun to move.

They were slithering and sliding around the pit walls and wrapping themselves around the wailing grotesques. There was a scraping noise as the stone snakes moved over the stone wall. Some of the snakes were even moving down towards the bottom of the pit. One reached the floor and made its way over towards Claudia, she was absolutely sure it was deliberately coming her way. The snake stopped directly in front of her, reared upwards and hissed at her as loud as it could. Claudia could see no way out this, she couldn't get out and the snakes were coming for her. She closed her eyes and waited.

Claudia knew she couldn't get out. The pit walls were too high and the snakes too many. She stood with her eyes closed and the noise of the crying grotesques all around her.

Then something shot by her shoulder. She thought it must have been one of the snakes attacking her but she hadn't felt anything bite her. Nervously she opened eyes and saw the most wonderful thing ever.

"You came" She shouted with delight.

"How could I not." Stonecat replied.

The cat was staring down the snake that had been threatening Claudia, baring his teeth menacingly. His back was arch and his tail was high in the air as he made himself as big as possible.

"Besides" He continued "I didn't come here alone. I've brought some friends."

Claudia looked up towards the rim of the pit. All around the edge there were the faces of the cat statues of York. They had come from all over the city; Kings Square, Pavement and Coppergate, a white cat from Low Petergate, brightly coloured cats from Ousegate and Friargate. Claudia even recognised the two black cats she had seen fighting near Mr Barry's house. There must have been nearly thirty cats in all. Above the noise of the grotesques, Claudia began to hear another sound. A low hum, not unlike the sounds of planes getting closer she had heard when speaking to Yves. This time, however, she realised it was the growling sound of a host of angry cats.

All of a sudden the growls became screeches as the cats began to attack. Jumping down all around them and making for the snakes. There was a tremendous noise of statues striking against statues and the cries of the individual snakes and cats.

"Look at them" The Master Mason screamed with excitement "Look at those magnificent cats. Such delicate carving. Brilliant and brave. They're here to save us. Such magnificent cats."

It was the first time that Claudia had seen The Master Mason look anything other than despairing and racked with guilt.

"Up there," Mathilda called out "They've got the ladder."

Claudia followed the pointed finger and saw what she meant. The two cats from The Shambles, one black and one made of wool, were dragging the rope ladder towards the edge of the pit with their teeth. As they reached the lip of the pit they dropped the ladder down for Claudia and the others to use.

"Quick let's get out of here." Mathilda cried.

"You two go." The Mason shouted back "These wonderful cats and I can cope here. Stonecat, fetch me my hammer and chisel."

Claudia and Mathilda climbed the rope ladder as Stonecat bounded out of the pit in search of the mason's hammer and the other cats fought the snakes down below. Claudia and Mathilda looked at each other.

"I think I know where we can find The Queen of Shadows." Claudia said.

She might have had a plan but they did not get far. The Whispering Shadows wouldn't let them.

Chapter 19 High Petergate

The Whispering Shadows swirled around the edges of the rounded interior of the tower that they stood inside.

"You're useless."

"I can't stand you"

"You're pathetic."
The voices were getting louder. Claudia felt frightened, angry and unable to stand up to the muttering. The shadows came closer and closer to where they were stood. Mathilda reached out and put her arm around Claudia, bringing her close to her in protection.

"How are we going to get out of this one?" Mathilda asked.

"I have no idea" Claudia replied.

THUMP. THUMP. THUMP.

Our armies obeyed our commands

We were lords of all we surveyed

"Unless…unless we can find some help from somewhere."

Were those thumps actually footsteps coming up the steps of Clifford's Tower.

THUMP. THUMP. THUMP.

And our swords still rest in our hands

Awaiting for those who need aid

They certainly sounded like footsteps. The footsteps of something heavy, coming slowly and deliberately up the steps in careful formation.

THUMP. THUMP. THUMP.

Carved by finest stonemasons

Ready for all that life brings

We stand with infinite patience

The Stone Carved Choir of Kings

The Kings came marching into the inside of the tower, three at a time with swords raised. They looked different to the last time she had seen them. The last time she saw them they were all plain white stone but now they were painted all different colours. Golds, silvers, reds, greens, blues and blacks.

The fifteen statues came to a stop in a line protecting Mathilda and Claudia. They all faced forwards without a hint of expression on their faces, not moving at all and completely blocking Mathilda and Claudia from the Whispering Shadows. The voices of the shadows grew louder and their swirling faster as if they were building towards and attack. Suddenly the Whispering Shadows shot forward towards Mathilda and Claudia but before they could reach them the Stone Carved Choir of Kings thrust their hands and swords up in protection. There was a loud clank as the Whispering Shadows crashed into the Choir of Kings and the shadows could not get through. They shadows retreated before trying another stack. Once again there was a clank and the Choir of Kings stood in protection of those that needed aid. There was another attack from the shadows and another resounding clank.

We stand with infinite patience

The Stone Carved Choir of Kings

They were safe and under no threat from the Whispering Shadows. They'd been saved by these statues carved long ago to provide hope to the people of York.

The coast was clear and they ran through the door of the tower and out of the castle.

Claudia and Mathilda raced through the streets of York. As they ran up Castlegate and Coney Street, Claudia explained to Mathilda all the details of her quest for the Peterkeys, finding the map of York with the clues in the key, solving each clue in turn and meeting Neville, Percy, Warwick the Dog, Etty the artist, Dr Snow, Queen Philippa, Yves the Airman and St. William. It was only as she said it all out loud that she realised just how much she had done. Mathilda spent the entire journey saying how impressed she was at Claudia's ingenuity and perseverance. By the time they reached the end of Blake Street, Claudia had just about brought Mathilda entirely up to speed with all that had happened.

They turned right onto Duncombe Place, a wide 19th Century road created to provide a sweeping route up to the west end of The Minster. However, before they reached The Minster they turned left onto High Petergate. Claudia felt like they had entered a tunnel, the narrow street lined with high buildings either side and the far end blocked by the impenetrably closed gateway of Bootham Bar. By the doors at the base of the bar was the sight that Claudia was hoping to see, one man dressed in bright white robes and one Queen of Shadows hovering on the ground and sucking in all the light from around her. They seemed to be struggling with something and they looked like they were arguing.

"What's wrong?" Mathilda called out "Isn't the key working properly?"

Balthazar and The Queen of Shadows looked around angrily.

"You two?" The Queen of Shadows called out "I thought you had been dealt with."

"You gave us the gold key." Balthazar shouted "Why isn't it working in this lock?"

"I gave you *a* gold key" Claudia replied "The thing is, I found that some souvenir shops sell fake keys that look really old. You can also go to hobby shop that sells art supplies to get some gold paint and before you know it, you've got yourself a gold key."

"We would have told you" Mathilda joined in "But you are The Queen of Shadows and you know everything."

"I have no time for this" The Queen of Shadows seemed emotional for the first time "I shall have to deal with you two myself."

Mathilda and Claudia glanced at each other. They both realised that they had been so distracted with catching up with the two others that they hadn't considered what would happen next.

"Run Claudia." Mathilda ordered and stepped forwards towards the Queen of Shadows.

Claudia tried to argue but thought better of it and began backing away towards the end of High Petergate. The Queen of Shadows glided across the ground towards them. Mathilda tried to block the passageway but was simply brushed aside and knocked to the floor.

"Make sure she does not get away." The Queen of Shadows barked towards Balthazar. "I'm going after the girl"

Claudia began to run away. The Queen of Shadows was gaining on her very quickly, there was no way that she would get away. She crossed over Duncombe Place and over towards St. Michael le Belfry Church. There were people there, two people. No, three people. They got out of her way but were they going towards the Queen of Shadows? Were they deliberately getting in the way? Claudia couldn't really tell, she just had to keep running. But whatever had happened the Queen of Shadows didn't seem to be gaining on her anymore.

Claudia kept running. She had no idea where she was going or what was going to happen but she knew she was scared. She couldn't think straight at all. It was like her mind was full of fog.

"Don't be afraid of the fog."

She didn't need to know what was going to happen in the end. She just needed to know what she was going to do next. She shouldn't be afraid of the fog. She could always change plans as the fog began to clear.

She reached the end of Stonegate and instinctively turned right knowing that the Queen of Shadows would follow her. She felt as if things were beginning to get clearer as she headed for an alleyway she knew would be on her left hand side. As she reached the end of the alleyway she checked back over her shoulder to see that The Queen of Shadows had obviously got away from those people and had definitely seen her go this way. Claudia felt like she knew exactly what to do now. She suddenly felt so grateful to whoever had got in the way of the Queen of Shadows, it had given her just the perfect amount of time to make a plan.

The other end of the alleyway led her out onto Swinegate. Claudia slowed her pace down and came to a stop around half way down the street, turned and waited for her pursuer to catch her up. Out of the alleyway came The Queen of Shadows, she looked angrier than before as well as looming larger than she had seemed before. She was still floating across the ground and still causing everything around her to turn black.

 "This is over" The Queen of Shadows declared "Give me the keys girl. The proper keys."

"You need to listen." Claudia attempted to reason.

"I do not need to listen. You need to give me the keys."

"Really, you need to listen." Claudia tried again.

There was a low rumble in the distance.

"I do not need to listen to anybody, I am The Queen of Shadows and I know all."

"You really would be better to listen"

Claudia felt like she was almost enjoying this. The rumble was increasing in volume as were the high pitched squeals that she could now hear.

"Why should I listen" The Queen of Shadows demanded.

"Because if you had listened, you'd have heard them."

As Claudia spoke she pointed behind The Queen of Shadows to the masses of pigs that had turned the corner into Swinegate and were almost upon them. As the first pigs reached them Claudia was just about able to jump into the entrance of the alleyway that Mathilda had called Mad Alice Lane. The Queen of Shadows had no time to do anything.

There was an almighty, otherworldly scream as the pigs engulfed the Queen of Shadows. Claudia saw a black cloud of shadows enter among the swine as they squealed and snorted their way along the road. As the mass of pigs moved forward, the shadow bounced around them getting smaller and smaller as the sound of the scream faded away. By the time the last pigs had passed the end of the alleyway the shadow was very small indeed and then there was nothing there. Nothing at all.

Claudia stepped out of the end of the alleyway, like the last time she had been down this way there was no sign that any pigs had ever been that way. But there was no sign of the Queen of Shadows either. It was as if she had just vanished.

Chapter 20 Stonegate

Mathilda and Balthazar heard The Queen of Shadows' scream all the way back in High Petergate. They had been struggling with each other, Mathilda desperate to try and get to Claudia's help whilst Balthazar was following orders to keep her where she was. However, once they had heard that scream it was clear that it was over one way or another and their fight seemed rather pointless. They looked at each other, nodded and sat down on the kerb waiting to see who would return to them.

"Why did you do it Balthazar?" Mathilda asked.

"Why do you think?" He replied.

"I don't know. Money? Power?"

"No. I thought she was right."

"The Queen of Shadows? You thought she was right." Mathilda sounded amazed at his response.

"Yes. I don't agree with her methods and I certainly don't agree that she is the only person that could save York but in one respect I thought she was right, York would be better off with keeping the doors locked and we should keep the echoes shut in only for those people that could appreciate them properly. If you let people in, they wipe out all of the echoes and history of the place and make this a worse place."

"But they decided years ago that locking the doors wasn't working. That's why the Peterkeys were spread around the city."

"Yes, but have you ever considered that they might have been wrong to do that?"

Mathilda was stopped in her tracks. Had she really thought hard as to why the keys were spread or whether it was the right thing to do? She thought back to her knowledge of the history of the city, how the closing of the gates stifled trade and innovation, how the removal of the Peterkeys allowed the city to flourish. The spread of the Echoes of York could only lead to more people being attracted to the city. People coming in to the city helped it grow, change and adapt to the modern world. The most important thing a city can do is find the balance between past, present and future. No, she concluded, it was definitely correct to keep the gates unlocked. But the fact that she had never thought about this before worried her.

All of that was academic now though, someone was coming around the corner and whoever it was this would be the end of it. Mathilda and Balthazar sat up straight, peering their heads around to see who it was that was coming their way.

"Claudia you clever, clever thing." Mathilda shouted out in excitement, jumping up and running towards her.

Balthazar's head slumped forward onto his chest and he let out a deep sigh. It was all over for him and he knew it. Slowly he stood up and walked towards them and offered himself up to Claudia and Mathilda. He looked defeated, as if all of the life had been knocked out of him.

"Come on." He said "Let's get this over with."

"I think we'll start off by taking you back to the castle prison cells" Mathilda informed him "See how you like spending some time in there."

The three of them walked towards the end of High Petergate, Mathilda leading the way with Balthazar shuffling along behind her."

"Fratres sumus non ipsa. Nos malon, nos malon."

The chanting was coming up towards them from their right hand side along Duncombe Place.

"Fratres, non sumus. Nos mendacium dicere."

Were these the Whitefriars? Claudia felt that she was getting better at picking out the differences between the groups. She looked to her right and saw the group of white robed men walking slowly up the street and chanting. She felt quite proud of herself.

"Come on Claudia." Mathilda called out to her "We haven't got time to stop and stare."

Claudia realised that she had indeed been staring at the friars who had virtually reached the end of High Petergate. She heard a voice beside her that snapped her out of her trance.

"Well it's been nice working with you but it time for me to go."

Claudia looked around and realised it had been Balthazar talking. He no longer looked defeated, instead he appeared to be back to his old self and if anything looked happy.

He pulled up the hood of his white robes, waved them a cheery goodbye and pushed his way into the centre of the group of friars. The rest of the group appeared to move and shift to allow him in without breaking stride or stopping their chanting.

Mathilda and Claudia could no longer tell which one was Balthazar. All of the men looked identical with their bright white robes and hoods covering their bowed heads.

"Fratres, non sumus. Nos mendacium dicere."

The friars kept going past the end of the road, chanting all the time.

"Quick, stop him. Stop them." Mathilda called out in panic.

The two of them rushed after the group and tried to push their way into the middle of them to find Balthazar. The friars were having none of it and Claudia felt the force of shoulders and elbows as they resisted her. She felt a heavy shove and fell to the ground.

"Fratres, non sumus. Nos mendacium dicere."

The friars were still marching forward and chanting. Claudia looked up from the floor and saw that they turned left towards a large metal gateway directly opposite the west doors of The Minster. Mathilda was still desperately trying to get amongst them, getting increasingly frantic at her failure. Finally she too fell to the floor as the last of the friars was making his way through the gateway. The gate slammed shut and they had gone.

Mathilda and Claudia lay on the floor looking at each other for a minute before Mathilda came over and picked Claudia off the floor.

"Have we lost him?" Claudia asked

"Yes we have. For now."

*

After they had got their breath back, Claudia explained to Mathilda about what had happened to the Queen of Shadows feeling a sense of pride as she spoke and then got a bit embarrassed when Mathilda was full of praise about what a brave, intelligent, wonderful person she was.

"There were some other people." Claudia said "Two or three, they seemed to stop her for a short time. I don't know who they were they were the perfect help."

"Oh I think you'd recognise them if you'd see them." Mathilda said smiling and pointing to three figures walking towards. They were all walking slightly gingerly as if they were had been hurt by what had happened.

Claudia looked up and squealed with delight.

"Lucy." She called out excitedly "Gus, Meg. What are you all doing here."
"We came to help" Meg replied with a slight grimace "We couldn't leave you to do this all alone."
"But how did you know?"
"We had our sources." Lucy joined in "You're not the only one who can investigate and search for things you know."

"Of course not. Silly me. And you stood up to the Queen of Shadows to help me. How can I ever repay you."
"It was nothing." Gus was the last to speak. "Anything to help out. Now if you'd just excuse me for a while. I think I need to sit down for bit."

Meg looked at him and shook her head.

"If you'd lose a bit of weight you'd be able to put up a better fight next time."

"Not now Meg hey. I just need a bit of a sit down. Hang on….next time?"

Claudia laughed. It was good to see them. So good. After thanking them again, Meg and Gus decided they were going to head back to the shop, Meg supporting her larger brother as they walked off shouting back over her shoulder that Claudia should come for a scone anytime she wanted. Mathilda and Lucy said that there were some people they needed to speak to about what had happened and after a little more praise suggested Claudia should go back to her mother and her own world.

She was going to do that but there was someone she needed to speak to first.

"You were absolutely magnificent." Claudia said

"Yes I was wasn't I." Stonecat replied.

Unlike Claudia, Stonecat did not seem at all embarrassed to be receiving praise. In fact, he seemed to enjoy every second of it.

"Were you hurt?" She asked.

"Some of us were hurt yes. But there was the strangest thing. There were all were fighting away cat vs. snake, I of course was tackling the most fearsome of the beasts, when all of a sudden we heard a horrible scream coming our way. With that, the snakes and the grotesques all stopped moving. Just froze where they were. The Master Mason says that now they aren't moving and not causing a threat to anyone, he will go about destroying all of the carvings. He says it is the least he can do given the circumstances. He also said that he knew people who would be able to fix up the injured cats so none of us will have any permanent injuries."

"Thank you again. I am so happy you came to help. And I worked out what it was that Balthazar had said that was worrying me. He knew that I was friends with Lucy Cavendish and he knew whereabouts in the city Mathilda had taken me before she went missing. I never told him any of that information. So he must have been following us or spying on us before Mathilda went missing. Once I realised that I knew he was in on the whole thing. That's why I needed your help. And we couldn't have done it without you. You are my hero."

"I had to come down and help. You mean too much to me. Now if you don't mind, I've got some serious napping to do."

Stonecat jumped up to his ledge and settled down as if he was about to go to sleep.

"Of course you do. I'll leave you to it." Claudia said before leaning in close to the cat "and I promise not to tell anyone you said something nice to me."

With that, Claudia felt there was nothing else to do but get back to her own world. She was surprised to find herself feeling excited about seeing her mother again. She made her way back to the library, swallowed hard and walked inside. She was delighted to find the inside busy with families and local people. She walked upstairs to the history section.

"There you are Claudia." Her mother called out "We lost you for a second. Not to worry you're here now. We've got to move on, time's a pressing."

The two of them went downstairs and out into the street. The routine of going about her normal Saturday in the busy centre filled Claudia with a sense of relief. No Queen of Shadows, no Peterkeys just boring old York.

She didn't even know she was doing it but found herself reaching out and taking her mother's hand as they walked along.

"What's this?" Her mother sounded surprised "I thought my grown up girl no longer held my hand."

The two of them smiled at each other. Claudia felt happy.

"Mum, who was Yves the Airman?" She asked innocently.

"Yves. Oh he saved the city."

"He saved the city of York? What did he do?"

"Well during the Second World War he flew fighter planes. He wasn't from round here of course, he was French, but he was stationed nearby. One night he saw that York was getting attacked by bombers and raced here to fight them off and protect the city. He was the first pilot to reach the city and by the time other brave pilots had reached here to join in the fight they had done enough to convince the attacking bombers to fly away from the city and end the attack. Who knows how much damage would have been done if it wasn't for Yves and the other pilots that night. You should have come to the talk I gave about him at the library, you'd have learned so much"

"He was a brave man then?"
"He had to be. He had to get on with things whether there was fog or smoke or whether he could see what was happening or not. He just had to get here and do everything he could to help the city. But just because we think of Yves as a brave hero, it doesn't mean that the men who were attacking the city should be thought of as evil villains."

"No." said Claudia in thought "They probably believed they were doing the right thing."

"Yes they probably did. Even if we now think they were badly wrong. That's a very mature way to look at things."

"Yes. It's like the men who Sir Thomas Fairfax stopped from smashing the stained glass windows at The Minster or who the men who William Etty stopped from destroying the city walls or who June Atkinson stopped pulling down historic buildings in the name of progress. At the time they thought they were doing the right thing."

"Yeesss." Claudia's Mother said narrowing her eyes in suspicion "You must have been doing a lot of reading in that library. You should start coming to my lectures."

"Mum." Claudia asked again. "What made you get interested in history?"

"Good question darling. I guess you can say that when I was about your age I had some very interesting friends."

Was that a look of recognition in her eyes? Claudia wondered who exactly her mother's friends might have been.

"What happened to your friends?" She asked curiously

"I don't know. I suppose I just stopped seeing them."

"Maybe." Claudia replied "Or maybe you just stopped looking."

Printed in Great Britain
by Amazon

63101417R00116